THE ORVILLE

SYMPATHY FOR THE DEVIL

SETH MacFARLANE

HYPERION AVENUE

LOS ANGELES   NEW YORK

Copyright © 2022 by 20th Television

All rights reserved. Published by Hyperion Avenue, an imprint of Buena Vista Books, Inc. No part of this book may be reproduced or transmitted in any form or by any means, electronic or mechanical, including photocopying, recording, or by any information storage and retrieval system, without written permission from the publisher. For information address Hyperion Avenue, 7 Hudson Square, New York, New York 10013.

First Digital Edition, July 2022
First Paperback Edition, October 2025

10 9 8 7 6 5 4 3 2 1
FAC-025438-25219

Printed in the United States of America

This book is set in Avenir and Chronicle
Designed by Amy C. King

Library of Congress Control Number: 2024949604

ISBN 978-1-368-10407-4
ISBN 978-1-368-09263-0 (ebook)
ISBN 978-1-368-09265-4 (audiobook)

The authorized representative in the EU for product safety and compliance is Disney Trading B.V., Asterweg 15S, 1031 HL, Amsterdam, The Netherlands
email: DCP.DL-EU.bookscontact@disney.com

www.HyperionAvenueBooks.com

SUSTAINABLE FORESTRY INITIATIVE Certified Sourcing

www.forests.org
SFI-01681

Logo Applies to Text Stock Only

PROLOGUE

The hotel was as luxurious as any high-end lodging that New York City had to offer. Founded by John Jacob Astor IV just a decade before, the nineteen-story French Beaux-Arts construct had, however, been somewhat controversial. It was built on Fifth Avenue, directly across from the opulent homes of the Vanderbilt family, which were doomed to be dwarfed by the towering height of the St. Regis. The Vanderbilts, along with a handful of other fabulously wealthy landowners, immediately set out to crush the project by any means possible: lawsuits alleging disturbance of the peace due to the blasting required for excavation, accusations of inadequate fireproofing, and even the suggestion that the hotel was in violation of early twentieth-century libation laws, which forbade the holding of a liquor license by any establishment within two hundred feet of a church. All attempts failed. The

5.5-million-dollar hotel opened to great fanfare on September 4, 1904. As the years passed, its prestige and popularity only grew more robust, and soon it had become a staple destination for convenience and comfort among business travelers and pleasure-seeking vacationers alike.

On this particular day, the opulent lobby crackled with energy, as guests and travelers hurried to and fro, bathed in the light of the elegant overhead chandeliers that as yet showed little tarnish. A calendar hung on the wall behind the front desk, displaying an intricate etching of well-to-do city dwellers strolling the paths of Central Park, beneath bold block type: APRIL 1914.

The clerk smiled as he offered a fountain pen to the man standing on the other side of the desk. "It's wonderful to have you with us again, Mr. Beechcroft. I hope you and your family have been in good health."

The well-heeled gentleman beamed with a prideful glow as he regarded his smartly dressed, freshly-scrubbed-looking wife, son, and daughter. "Please," he said with a rich but gentle baritone, "the pleasure is all ours. At this point, I wouldn't dream of staying anywhere else in the city."

"Even if he wanted to, I wouldn't let him," his wife chimed in.

Mr. Beechcroft took his cue. "Now you know who runs the household." A warm chuckle rippled through the group: patrons and manager enjoying an easy, benign familiarity.

"Don't worry," said the clerk, with a playful wink to Mrs. Beechcroft. "Your secret is safe with me."

"We stayed at the Plaza two years ago just to sample something new, and I must say, we—"

A wave of murmurs interrupted the man's frivolous entry into the frivolous exchange. Everyone turned at the sound of the commotion. In the entryway, a frantic, desperate-looking woman pushed past an indignant bellman, half running, half stumbling toward the reception area. Her apparel suggested generous wealth, with a fitted, high-waisted dress trimmed with frothy passementerie, elbow-length sleeves and long gloves, topped with a large hat featuring a deep crown.

No one was paying any attention to her finery. What caught the crowd's interest was the bundle she held in her arms.

It was an infant.

Swaddled in soft pale-lavender fabric, the child flitted his gaze about with the combined mixture of curiosity and fear that all newborn babies seem to exhibit. There was, however, no confusion about the mother's expression: terror. She moved to the center of the grand lobby, her eyes darting about with visible panic. She quickly scanned the bevy of nonplussed patrons, evidently searching for something, or someone . . . so it seemed. At last, she set her manic sights on the clerk behind the front desk, and barreled toward him. The clerk and the surrounding onlookers all reacted with expressions of stunned surprise as she attempted to deposit the child into his arms.

"Please!" she cried, hands trembling, eyes wet. "Take my baby!"

"Excuse me?" The clerk tried to resist the forced offering, gently pushing back, but the woman was implacable.

"Please, take him! Keep him safe!"

"Ma'am, who are you?"

"Please, I'm begging you!" Fiercely persistent, the woman pushed the infant across the countertop so that the clerk had no choice but to receive it.

"Ma'am, can you please tell me what's—"

But the woman ignored him. Her green eyes blazed like emeralds as she brushed quivering fingertips against her baby's cheek. "I love you," she said with a heated whisper. "With all my heart. And I'll come back for you. Do you hear me? *I'll come back.*"

The clerk now spoke with a more firm tone. "I need you to tell me what's going on—"

"Take care of him." What should have been a desperate plea in fact sounded more like a barked order. Her fiery gaze implied that, should the clerk falter in his new and unsolicited role as the boy's caretaker, there would be dire consequences. For now, however, she allowed herself one last longing glance at her abandoned offspring, her mind doing its utmost to take and preserve a permanent, clear-eyed snapshot despite the emotional fog of the moment.

And then at last, bringing a cool burst of air gusting in through the gilded front doors, she was gone.

—— ✧ ——

"She didn't even tell me what his name is," said the clerk, still cradling the infant in his arms. The child was now blissfully slumbering, completely unaware of the drama unfolding around him in the small, cramped office. The incommodious, utilitarian room shared few features with the resplendent lobby mere steps away. Three other members of the St. Regis's staff hovered over the sleeping baby, expressions of concern and curiosity etched on their faces.

"Maybe he hasn't got a name," said the concierge.

"Harry, what am I supposed to do with him?" said the clerk. "There's no way I can keep him. My mother is still sick, and I can barely take care of *her.*"

"There's always the orphanage," offered the bellman.

The maid grunted out a guttural blat of derision. "You can't leave him there. Have you ever seen the insides of those places? They're rat-infested prisons is what they are. He'd be better off if you just dumped him on the street." Then, a flicker of inspiration ignited in her eyes. "Wait a minute," she said. "What about the Vogels?"

The bellman raised an eyebrow as he lit up a cigarette. "Well now, *there's* an inspired idea."

The concierge appeared left out. "Who are the Vogels?"

"They're the couple staying in 1207," answered the bellman. "They're in from Berlin, and they, ah . . ." He paused and glanced at the maid. She dutifully took the baton:

"One of the girls overheard Mrs. Vogel and her husband talking last week. They . . . recently lost a baby."

"Oh my goodness," uttered the clerk. "That's horrible. How?"

"Typhoid."

"Oh, Lord. Those poor, poor people."

"I wonder . . ." mused the maid, "I wonder if we should ask them."

The concierge, who had been leaning casually on the edge of the accounting desk, suddenly rose to his full height. "That," he warned, "is not a wise notion."

"Why not?" said the maid, whirling to face him.

"If you do that, you're admitting to eavesdropping. I know you're trying to help, but if they take it the wrong way, you could lose your job."

The maid appeared undeterred. "I'm willing to take the gamble."

"So am I," said the clerk.

The gamble turned out to be a good one. Thus, the maid and the clerk stood back and smiled with the beaming aspect of a team of carpenters or painters immediately following the completion of time-consuming work. The Vogels were an unassuming but kindly-looking couple who appeared to be in their mid-thirties. Gunter and Ilse Vogel, he with sandy brown hair and a plump physique, she with a lighter shade and a trimmer figure, sat close to each other on the flowered sofa, gazing down at the stirring child whom she now held. Ilse's eyes sparkled with fresh tears as she spoke in heavily accented but nonetheless fairly fluent English.

"He is so very beautiful," she cooed. "The most precious child in the world. It has been such a long time waiting for this day. Whoever may doubt that the Lord hears all prayers . . . should only look into the eyes of this miracle."

Gunter appeared to suddenly remember that he and his wife were not alone in the suite. He glanced up at his benefactors. "What you have done for us . . . it will be impossible to repay. How can we ever thank you for this?"

"Don't thank us." The clerk smiled. "You said it yourself. God has blessed you. Thank *Him.*"

"The boy came to us with no name," the maid chimed in. "Not that it's our business, but I'd love to know . . . do you have any thoughts at all about what you might call him?"

Gunter and Ilse Vogel exchanged a pair of resolved grins. "We decided long ago," he shared, "that if we ever had a boy, we would name him Otto. After my father."

"I wish he were alive now," said Ilse. "To see for himself. He would be so proud to share his name with you . . . Otto." The infant's eyes fixated quizzically on his new mother as she spoke. "He will have the best life we can give him. He will be educated and cared for, but most of all, he will be loved. And he will grow up to be a good man. God bless Otto."

"God bless Otto," said Gunter.

CHAPTER ONE

"Zum Geburtstag viel Glück! Zum Geburtstag viel Glück! Zum Geburtstag alles gut! Zum Geburtstag viel Glück!"

The air popped and crackled with applause as the mighty little expulsion from Otto Vogel's lungs blew out the seven candles on his birthday cake.

"Ahhhh, *gut*! Job well done!" Gunter exclaimed.

The cake sat atop a small wooden picnic table, encircled by colorfully wrapped gifts, all dappled by sunlight filtering through the trees in the green front yard of the Vogels' modest Berlin residence. The seven or eight other children present maintained varying degrees of attentiveness, some staring intently at the unopened prizes, others darting about on the grass, playing a chaotic game of tag. In addition to the other parents, Gunter and Ilse were joined by Gunter's sister, Heidi, and her husband Karl, as well as Ilse's brother, Carsten. Heidi and Karl appeared fully engaged in the festivities. Carsten, however, stood removed from the whole affair, quietly draining a mug of dark beer as he stood leaning against an oak tree.

"There's no luckier birthday boy than the son of a baker!" Heidi smiled as she indicated the lavishly adorned cake. It was true. The thick chocolate interior was sweetly clothed in a fudge frosting lovingly fringed with multi-hued, edible sugar embroidery. Yes, Gunter's culinary handiwork was surely a catnip for juvenile taste buds.

Gunter's establishment had prospered before the war, enjoying a reputation as one of the finest bakeries in Berlin, so much so that it had had to expand its capacity in order to accommodate the mushrooming demand from the commu-nity. He and Ilse had in fact been quite well-to-do—that is until after the war, when they were quickly and mercilessly crippled by the postwar hyperinflation. They had not been completely wiped out or pauperized like so many other Germans, but nonetheless this once-affluent business owner could now be seen scrambling to stay afloat, which meant moving to a much more modest home, no expensive vaca-tions in fine hotels, and fewer birthday offerings. However, the baked goods remained splendid. "We may be poorer," Gunter would often say, "but the chocolate is still rich!"

Ilse regarded the sparse candles jutting upward from the mostly unpierced frosting on the cake's surface. "If only they could stay this young forever," she said.

"Mama, can I open the rest of my presents?" asked Otto

hopefully, his little hands slapping at the tabletop with excited, ungraceful gestures.

Ilse laughed. "Yes, of course you can."

Heidi handed him a rectangular gift wrapped in crimson paper, with a little yellow bow on top. "Here. This is from Karl and I."

Though he was too young to fully comprehend his feelings, Otto's developing brain was still able to appreciate the emotionally pungent intensity of that brief moment when the tearing of the wrapping had begun, but the interior mystery had not yet been revealed. It was a sensation more intoxicating perhaps even than the reveal itself. His short baby-carrot fingers began shredding the paper with delighted abandon.

Karl chuckled. "He attacks his gifts like a soldier breaking down the walls of a fortress."

"Indeed," Gunter responded, a tone of pride in his voice.

"Keep that up, Otto, and you'll have a bright future in the army."

As Otto pulled the shiny, red toy airplane from the discarded wrapping, like a mechanical reptile shedding its molted skin, the light, convivial atmosphere was broken by an audible belch from beneath the oak tree.

"A bright future," muttered Carsten, tonelessly. His weighted, gray expression was profoundly out of place in the midst of the merriment. He appeared to know this, and that appeared to be the point. "Perhaps you would describe his future for us. In the army, you say?" There was a slight drunken wobble in his step as he emerged from beneath the shadow of the tree, a grim, invasive presence encroaching upon the celebration.

Had an outsider observed Carsten's emergence into the sunlight, they would now clearly have seen what they might have missed before: a loose, empty sleeve flapping lazily over the stumpish remains of half an arm—an ugly memento of the war.

"It was . . . a joke," Karl offered with a benign half smile.

"A joke," Carsten mocked, ambling ever closer to the group. "That is fitting. Just like the German army, hm? A joke."

"Carsten," Ilse said, glowering at him, "today is not the day."

"Ah, I see. And what about tomorrow? Or the day after?" Carsten trained a black stare on Karl, who looked to be at a loss for diplomatic options. "You speak of a bright future for Otto. Where? Where will this bright future unfold? In this ruined country?"

"Please forgive my brother, Karl," Ilse interjected, placing a gentle hand on Karl's wrist. "He's still fighting for the Kaiser."

Carsten stumbled backward with showy outstretched arms and exaggerated indignation. *"Fighting?"* He spat out something that could either have been a laugh or a retch. "Oh no. No, there is no fight. Not anymore. Versailles has taken care of that. The British and the French have seen to it quite efficiently. They have caged Germany like an animal in a zoo. And we have allowed it!" His eyes narrowed. *"For now. For now, we have allowed it."*

Gunter rose, seemingly having had enough of the disruption. "What do you mean? The war is over, Carsten. You would do well to join us here in the 1920s. We are moving onward. There will never be another war like the one we've just been through. Humanity has learned its lesson."

"So has Germany, it seems," replied Carsten, kicking a fallen twig out of his path as he took another step toward the table. "That is, if men like you command the day. How easily you bow to your new overlords. I remember when you loved your country."

"I still do," Gunter snapped.

"You disguise it well."

"If you see a friend or a brother whom you truly love destroying himself, you do not feed his undoing through blind fealty. You try to save him from it. It's the same with one's country, Carsten. True patriotism is not only to celebrate your nation's glories, but to care for her if she begins to decay. To fight the deterioration. In Germany's case, to help her learn to live in peace. That is the only way she will truly prosper."

"Passionate words for a baker," Carsten said, his voice dripping with disdain. "You speak of brothers? Two million of your brothers were killed fighting for their homeland. For your homeland. While you made bread." Carsten let the word hang in the air as if it were a profanity. "And you dare to call them sinners."

Gunter did not take the bait. "It's Otto's seventh birthday," he said with stony defiance. "I would like him to remember it fondly. Go home, Carsten."

The confrontation had evidently concluded. Otto turned his full attention to the gleaming wings of his new toy.

The bread rose to a rich golden brown inside the envelope of heat generated by the baker's oven, its doughy surface slowly texturing itself until it resembled a tundra seen from afar. As the door opened, the trapped heat waves rushed to escape the confines of their cell, dissipating with a gentle burst that briefly bathed Gunter's graying features in cinnamon-scented warmth. With a pair of thick mitts, Gunter slowly removed the bread from the oven, placed it gently on the counter, then carefully began wrapping it in a white cloth, as if he were a doctor tending to a newborn.

The bakery itself was a compact treasure trove of breads, muffins, cakes, pies, tarts, cookies, pretzels, and all manner of sweetened pastries. It was a Garden of Eden for a young boy of seventeen with a healthy, rapidly growing body constantly hungering for fuel to maintain its biological expansion. As Otto munched with pleasure on a small sugar cake, he regularly glanced at his father, making sure the old man was still immersed in his work, unaware of the confectionary thievery taking place under his nose. Suddenly, Gunter looked up. Caught, Otto quickly turned away and crammed the remainder of the treat into his mouth, all in one smooth motion.

Too late. Gunter straightened with a deep scowl, accentuating the wrinkles and crevices that the years had carved into his features. "Otto! *No more cakes!* Mein Gott, you're going to bankrupt us!"

"I'm only eating the stale ones," the boy carped through a mouthful of crumbling Anispläzchen.

"There *are* no stale ones!" his father snapped. "What kind of a shop do you think I run? Now come take this loaf. Frau Schneider is expecting it by five o'clock." He finished sealing up the warm Weißbrot and slid it across the counter toward Otto.

"Yes, Papa," the boy grumbled, the usual grim feeling of penal servitude taking hold as he sullenly scooped the parcel into his arms. He had never cared for this business, beyond the consumption of baked goods. He had no desire to one day accept stewardship of the establishment, as his father expected. He knew how long the hours were, and how hard his father had to work to keep it going. He believed he was born for grander destinies.

Gunter passed him a small handful of coins. "Here. That's only to make change if she needs it. Don't come back with magazines and candy like you did last time."

"Can I go to the Tiergarten with Jurgen afterward?"

"I don't like Jurgen. He smokes."

"*I* don't smoke."

"Good, keep it that way."

"So . . . can I go?"

Gunter sighed. "All right. Make the delivery, and then you can go see your friend."

"Thank you, Papa."

Otto hurried off. You never knew when the old man would change his mind.

The Kurfürstendamm was bustling with activity beneath the bright Berlin sunshine. Otto knew he could have taken a shorter route to Frau Schneider's house, but he liked to be surrounded by the energy of Berlin's liveliest avenue, a world away from the stifling confines of his dreary home. Despite the ongoing depression, the symptoms of which were evident (beggars, unemployed veterans, and prostitutes—female and male—all openly soliciting), Otto saw only the sights, sounds, and smells of infinite opportunity, and the promise of a future in which anything was possible. For him, 1931 was surely the precursor to a glorious new era.

Otto ambled along with no particular urgency to his step, and paused at the window of a candy shop, his eye drawn to the dazzling array of sweets on display within: chocolate bars, licorice, caramels, and a big jar of Gummibärchen. He gazed intently for a moment at the sugary cornucopia, his sandy brown hair ruffling lightly in the afternoon breeze. He reached into his pocket, and pulled out the Reichsmark his father had given him, bouncing them gently in his palm with nervous indecision. Surely one Riesen or a single licorice stick would be all right . . . but no, his father was as thorough and precise as a banker when it came to money. The verbal lashing he would receive would hardly be worth the brief pleasure the confection would afford his eager taste buds. He stuffed the coins back into his pocket.

As he turned to proceed along his route, a shadow fell across his face. Spinning on his heel, he saw that the sun was blocked by two boys, both larger and slightly older than Otto. One was taller than the other, but both dwarfed him with inches to spare. They wore expressions of sneering superiority, making it evident they'd decided they had business with him. Otto felt a little spurt of adrenaline course through his body as it went on confrontational high alert, knowing that a quick and easy exit was unlikely.

"What's in your pocket?" said the taller of the two boys.

"What?" Otto answered limply, though he'd heard the question.

"I saw you put something in your pocket."

"Oh. It's—it's nothing." He moved to evade them, but the larger boy stepped directly into his path, forcing him against the front window of the clockmaker's shop next door. "Ja? Nothing? Let's see."

With a somewhat pleading gesture, Otto indicated his white cloth bundle. "I have to deliver this bread to Frau Schneider." He attempted to sidestep the boys in the opposite direction, but the shorter one grabbed his arm. "Oh no, not yet."

"Hey! Let me go! Stop!" Otto tried to wrench himself loose as the taller boy grasped his other arm, twisting it behind his back. It wasn't painful, but he was solidly restrained, unable to break free. He squirmed with all his might, trying to shake them off with spastic bursts of body movement, but the boys were stronger.

"Hold him still!" the taller one barked as he thrust his hand roughly into Otto's pocket, snatching at the coins. He opened his palm to examine the confiscated treasure. "Ohh, look at this," he snarled cruelly. "He lied to us."

"Give that back!" cried Otto, reaching out to grasp the boy's hand, which quickly and deftly hooked behind his back. "Give it back!"

"Or what?" The shorter one grinned with malice. He shoved Otto to the ground, hard. Otto landed on his behind with a thud, the impact jostling the parcel from his arms. The bread loaf tumbled out of the wrap and onto the sidewalk. The taller boy reached down and savagely tore a chunk from the top side, taking a big, greedy bite. "You're the baker's boy, ja? Tell your father I prefer strawberry pie."

Suddenly, the front door of the clockmaker's shop swung open, and a well-dressed, white-bearded man of about sixty strode out with surprising spryness, aggressively inserting himself into the midst of the conflict. "Hey! You boys! Get out of here! Right now!"

The boys backed away obediently, but the persistent smirks on their faces betrayed an underlying indifference to the man's authority, as if they were retreating only because it suited them in the moment.

"Guten Tag, Herr Hirschbock," said the shorter boy, his tone dripping derision.

"Go on!" the man snapped. "Go! Before I call your parents!"

"Look at the poor little boy," sneered the taller one. "He needs a wrinkly old Jew to protect him." They cackled malignantly, and at last turned to depart. As the ugly staccato of their cachinnation receded into the general clamor of the Kurfürstendamm, Herr Hirschbock moved to help Otto to his feet.

"Are you all right, Otto?" he asked, brushing dirt off the boy's pants and shirtsleeves. Otto felt the pressuring choke of a sob pushing itself up from the back of his throat. He wasn't in pain, but rather humiliated. "Yes, I'm fine," he managed to answer with just a slight quiver, his resolve stiffening to avoid the further embarrassment of tears in public.

"Did they hurt you?"

Otto bitterly shook off the gentle ministrations of the old clockmaker, and scooped up the now-ruined remains of his parcel. "No, I'm not hurt." It was true. He had been lucky, although he knew from past experience that he was an exceptionally tough boy in the physical sense, making up in resilience for what he lacked perhaps in stoutheartedness. He wished, however, that he had had the courage and bravery to stand up for himself. In the recesses of his mind, he feared the boys were right. He *had* required the assistance of the old Jew to bail him out of his predicament. He felt weak and ashamed. Eschewing anything like a thank-you, he hurried away from Herr Hirschbock back toward the bakery, and the assured wrath of his father.

As he ambled up the street toward home, he became aware of a thunderous commotion emanating from a nearby beer hall. It was customary for the large pubs to play host to noisy crowds, but there was something unusual about the cadence of the ruckus. It was rhythmic, pulsating. He could hear the faint bellow of a single voice, followed repeatedly by the boisterous roar of a male throng. As he drew closer, he noticed a small group of three or four Braunhemden, the "brown shirts." He recognized the standard uniform of the paramilitary branch of the rising Nazi party. Before he could inquire about the source of the uproar, one of the young men addressed him.

"Did you do battle with a duck?"

Confused, Otto stared dumbly for a moment, then

realized he was still holding the destroyed loaf in view, its crust showing the ragged laceration from his encounter with the young toughs.

"Oh … no, I …" He regarded the strong, confident-looking Sturmabteilung. "I was in a fight." He felt guilty for the lie, knowing he had done nothing to defend himself during the one-sided confrontation.

"Ah," said the young Nazi, taking him at his word. "Well, times have been hard. We do our best to survive, yes?"

Otto nodded silently, unable to offer a response that wouldn't make him sound childish and stupid.

"But things are changing," declared one of the other young men, with certitude. "*Germany* is changing."

"Why are they cheering?" asked Otto, peering past them to get a glimpse inside the hall.

The first man smiled at him. "Would you like to find out?"

Otto entered the packed beer hall, to find a great many more Braunhemden inside, along with some civilians and even several women. There were chairs and tables generously laden with large mugs of rich, dark beer. Most of the spectators, however, were standing. Their attention was raptly focused on a red-faced, bellowing orator with short blond hair and a hawk nose who addressed the crowd with great passion. He wore a uniform similar to the others, but he looked to be somewhat more decorated. Otto knew little about the hierarchy of the Braunhemden, but basic observation indicated that the speaker outranked his audience. The man spoke in clipped, precise tones.

"With the sadistic and savage Treaty of Versailles, England and France gleefully took their butcher knives to our great land! It is said that if you strike at a king, you must kill him! A German is the same! If you wound a German and you do not kill him, he will rise again with twice the might! Twice the power! And he will vanquish you without mercy!"

There was something intoxicating, something electric about the atmosphere in this room. Otto drew closer as the man plowed onward, drilling his way through the speech with blunt efficiency. "The Führer has given us back our might! Our dignity! And our rightful place as the greatest nation on Earth! Under his leadership, the National Socialists will claim the Fatherland, and we will seek out our enemies and destroy them! The Bolshevik, the Jew, the conspirators who dared to oppress us, and all of those who stabbed our army in the back in the last war! They will be crushed under the heel of our great movement, with the heavens guiding the hand of our Führer! Sieg!"

"Heil!" the men thundered in unison.

"Sieg!" the speaker called out.

"Heil!" answered the men.

"Sieg!" shouted the speaker.

"Heil!" Otto joined in.

CHAPTER TWO

O tto's gaze swept across the grandiose ballroom, as the liquid ebb and flow of colorful bodies danced by with champagne-fueled sparkle. Although the swastika-emblazoned banners that hung high on the walls dominated the decor, the presence of a multitude of nationalities was evident: Italian, English, Swiss, Spanish, Danish, Hungarian, Belgian, and a few others Otto did not recognize. There were ambassadors, politicians, military attachés, and of course SS and other officers of the Nazi Party. He marveled at the rapid transformation that had occurred since Hitler had become firmly entrenched as the leader of Germany. As promised, he had restored the nation's greatness, as evidenced by the show of power assembled in this room. Successfully making a mockery of the fear-mongering, alarmist histrionics of the foreign press, Hitler had done a marvelous job of reclaiming Germany's historic lands and positioning the country for further expansion while expertly keeping the peace, despite the absurd predictions of the journalists.

Otto felt supremely fortunate to be among those in attendance at the sumptuous affair, courtesy of his good friend Heinz Fischer, who had extended the invitation. The two felt like the lords of creation as they strolled the soiree in their smartly pressed SS uniforms, a pair of rising standouts seemingly destined for long, prosperous careers.

"I wish my uncle could be here," remarked Otto with a prideful smile. "He would be ecstatic. He fought in 1914."

"Infantry?" asked Heinz, sipping his champagne.

"Ja."

"So did my father."

As if smarting from the quick, sharp sting of an old injury, a wincing expression flitted swiftly across Otto's face. "I wish I could say the same," he muttered, glancing absently at a pair of naval attachés engaged in a friendly debate of some variety.

"Your father didn't serve?" Heinz inquired.

Otto couldn't tell from his expression whether he was silently judging the son for the sins of the father. Anxious, however, to distance himself from the old man's embarrassing patriotic deficiencies, he answered quickly. "Oh yes, he served. He served *dessert*. He was a baker."

"Well . . . you can't fight a war on an empty stomach," Heinz replied with a wry grin. Otto was quietly grateful for his friend's light tone.

"*He* certainly didn't."

Heinz gave him a supportive slap on the back. "He must be very proud of *you* though, no?"

"Hardly. We haven't spoken in five years. He's too blind to see what Hitler has done for Germany. He'd rather we remained a punching bag for the Allies."

But Heinz appeared not to be listening. Instead, his gaze was fixed upon the far corner of the hall. Otto turned to look. Beside a long table decked out with a glorious array of pastries that put his father's paltry efforts to shame, Otto beheld an even more glorious sight. Three women laughed gaily over some shared joke as they nibbled from a multi-tiered platter of chocolate scones. Two were pleasantly handsome, perhaps in their early fifties, but the third . . .

Otto felt the rushing tide of instant longing as it surged through his bloodstream. She was blonde, perhaps twenty years old, with piercing blue eyes and a stunningly magnetic, heaven-sent smile that looked as if it could and must be her permanent expression. She threw her head back as she laughed, accentuating an elegant jawbone that Michelangelo would envy. Who she was Otto had no idea. Perhaps Heinz knew.

"I've only seen her once before," he said, "at a reception for the Danish ambassador. But I never learned her name."

As Otto pondered the seemingly Herculean challenge of wrangling a formal introduction to this magnificent creature, and the likely reality that such a woman must surely be spoken for, an unfamiliar voice jolted him back to reality. "I trust you boys are enjoying yourselves?"

He turned to find himself face-to-face with a formidable-looking SS general. Instantly, both he and Heinz snapped to attention, their bootheels clicking and their arms shooting skyward in salute to the superior officer.

"Heil Hitler!" the boys barked out in unison.

"Heil Hitler," the general responded, with what sounded like a trace of amusement. He addressed Heinz, gesturing to Otto. "And who might this be?" Otto realized that his friend was already acquainted with the man.

Heinz answered crisply, "Oberjunker Otto Vogel. This is my commanding officer, General Schmidt."

"An honor, sir," said Otto, with a deferential tilt of the head. "I was humbled when Heinz offered the invitation."

"Yes, rather unorthodox to be sure, however I'm sure Heinz told you of my little . . . idiosyncrasy."

"He did, sir. It is our good fortune."

As Heinz had informed him, General Schmidt always tried to sneak a few low-ranking SS officers into these high-profile gatherings. It was his belief that an occasional first-hand glimpse of the glory enjoyed by those who dedicated their lives to the SS and the Party—and faithfully endured the long, slow climb through its hierarchy—would further fuel the loyalty and conviction of the up-and-comers. It was tacitly understood that those who lucked into this special privilege would return to their peers with glowing accounts of the experience, which would trickle down through the ranks, where they would fortify a thicker membrane of loyalty. So, here they were, two SS officer candidates in their mid-twenties, getting a taste of the high life.

"I see you have been . . . admiring the view." For a moment, Otto was confused by the remark. Then suddenly, he felt the blood rushing to his cheeks as he realized what the general meant. He had observed their interest in the blonde girl's comely face and lithe figure.

"Oh . . . y-yes, sir," Otto sputtered lamely.

"Quite lovely." The general smiled.

"Yes, sir."

"So, tell me . . ." The general idly wiped smooth a small wrinkle in his lapel with two fingers. "What would you do with a woman like that, hm?"

Heinz and Otto looked at each other, nervously. Otto had the acute sensation that he was being toyed with for some as-yet-unclear reason. He was grateful when Heinz spoke first. "I think that I would . . . put her on a pedestal every day. . . ." Then with a jovially lascivious glint, "And haul her down at night!" Otto's eyes widened. Such a ribald attempt at humor was a bold gamble.

At first it seemed to pay off, as the general chuckled gamely, but almost immediately Otto registered an odd sub-layer to his expression. "Well, you know what our friends the Italians say," the general quipped. "Only peasants make love at night." To Otto's dismay, the general then turned his attention to him. Not off the hook after all. "And what about you, young man?"

"Sir?" Otto stalled.

"What would you do with a woman like that?"

He felt himself beginning to sweat. Was this, in fact, merely man-to-man verbal horseplay, or was he being tested in some fashion? For lack of a better option, he chose wide-eyed honesty. "I would . . . I would ask her to marry me."

The general seemed genuinely amused and delighted by this response, his laugh far warmer than it had been with Heinz. "Marry you!" he repeated, a slight bounce in his dominating stance. "Don't you think you should meet her first?"

"Meet her . . . ?"

He glanced at Heinz, but the other boy was just as perplexed.

The general suddenly called across the room with the round-toned projection one would expect from an officer of such rarefied rank. *"Annelise! Come here!"*

The woman immediately glided across the room with cheerful confidence, filling Otto with a mix of exhilaration and panic as she approached. He had the distinct sensation of standing on a railroad track, watching a powerful locomotive rushing toward him, and he had to fight the urge to get out of the way. He hoped his perspiration wasn't too visible. The general wrapped an arm around the girl's waist and beamed with pride as he introduced her. "I would like you to meet my daughter, Annelise. These are Lieutenants Heinz Fischer and Otto Vogel."

"A pleasure," she said. Her voice was a surprisingly smooth, velvety, self-assured alto that only exacerbated

Otto's schizophrenic impulses to feel the caress of those soft, ivory arms, and at the same time to be anywhere else but inside this socially petrifying circle of discourse. "How do you know my father?" she asked as she tossed an adoring look upward at the imposing man, whose return glance appeared more docile than any SS would have seemed capable of, let alone one of the general's rank.

"I . . . have the honor of serving under his command," Heinz managed to say.

"You're very fortunate." She smiled. "And you, Herr Vogel?"

Otto opened his mouth, and to his horror, nothing came out. He surely must have resembled the subject of Edvard Munch's disturbing contribution to the vulgar movement of Proto-Expressionism. What was it called? *The Scream*?

"I . . ." But that single little droplet of sound was apparently all that his dry pipes would offer.

"Otto and I have just met," the general said, bailing him out. "However, he has been quite forthcoming when sharing his interests."

"Oh really?" she answered with curiosity. "Such as?"

"The sacred institution of matrimony, for example." Otto wanted to die. But the general pressed onward with waggish delight. "Tell me, Herr Vogel, what do you think of my Annelise? Do you still want to marry her?"

"I do," said Otto, as she gently slid the gold ring onto his finger.

CHAPTER THREE

"And do you, Annelise Schmidt, take Otto Vogel to be your lawfully wedded husband, to have and to hold, from this day forward, for richer, for poorer, in sickness and in health, to love and to cherish, till death do you part, according to God's holy ordinance?"

"I do," she replied, and though Otto had come to know this woman deeply since that fateful day on which her beauty had rendered him verbally flaccid, and though his heart now beat more with love than with lust, in that moment he felt a wonderful electric burst of the same out-of-body vertigo that he had experienced when she had first come gliding across that floor and into his life, which she had transformed in the most unexpected and exhilarating way.

He slid the ring onto her finger. The elderly clergyman smiled as if this were the only true union over which he had ever presided. "Then, in the name of the Father, the Son, and the Holy Spirit, I now pronounce you man and wife. You may kiss the bride."

The crowd of guests applauded warmly, the sound reverberating back in on itself courtesy of the carved stone walls of the elegant old church. Heinz, the best man, looked on with a wide grin as Otto kissed his new bride. As he tasted the sweet, familiar lips, he silently thanked God for bestowing such good fortune upon him. It truly was a precious gift to find love and take it all the way to the altar.

The reception was an outdoor affair, and the mild weather was just right. An array of sumptuously decked-out tables dotted the green grass just adjacent to the church, with large canopies providing shade. Waiters in white jackets were pouring wine for those already seated as the bride and groom strode in to another round of cheers. The couple waved enthusiastically to the assembled guests as Heinz approached with a beaming Ilse on his arm.

"Look at this. I picked up a date," he said rakishly, giving Ilse a peck on the cheek.

"Mama." Otto smiled, embracing his mother. "Isn't this weather grand?"

"It could not be more perfect," she agreed. "It was such a magnificent ceremony. Annelise, you looked so marvelously beautiful."

"Thank you, Frau Vogel," she said, giving Ilse's hand an affectionate squeeze. "It's a shame Herr Vogel couldn't be here as well."

Otto and Ilse exchanged an uncomfortable glance at Annelise's remark, and Otto's tone suddenly turned chilly. "Yes. A shame."

"He is sorry to miss this day," said Ilse gamely. "But . . . well, you know. His feelings have not changed."

"It's disgraceful," Otto shot back. "His only son's wedding."

"He is a man of strong convictions. And he is your father. I wish you could dignify him with a bit of respect for that, at least. For our family's sake."

"Mama," Otto replied sternly, "he has eyes. He must see what's happening in Germany. He must feel the renewed sense of pride. Of hope! Mein Gott, he's still a German!"

"He doesn't see the world as you do," she said quietly. Otto guessed she was conscious of prying ears, but he did not care. He knew he was right. If she continued to act as an apologist for Gunter's outdated—and downright dangerous—views, she ought to defend him at full voice. "Your father is either very stubborn . . . or very wise."

"Or very stupid."

Ilse looked as if someone had thrown a cold drink at her. For a brief moment Otto regretted his bluntness—he had never, in all their debates, been so openly insulting when it came to the old man, but damn it anyway. Times were changing. And old Gunter would have to reform his views . . . or . . . well, Otto had no control over the consequences.

"How . . . how could you say such a thing?" his mother replied, a catch in her throat. Annelise observed the exchange with the curious look of a child examining a carnival oddity.

"Because it's true," Otto answered evenly.

"Frau Vogel," Heinz interjected with a calm, diplomatic air, "Germany is on the rise. We've reclaimed the Rhineland, Czechoslovakia, Austria . . . there's even talk of Poland."

Ignoring him, Ilse kept her now steely gaze fixed on her son. "Your father does not believe in war for conquest. And . . ." She paused, as if contemplating whether to cross some invisible line. "And I happen to agree with him."

This time, both Heinz and Annelise wore expressions of bafflement.

"There is no limit to what we can achieve." Otto's voice had grown more full-bodied and decidedly icy. "And one day soon, Father will have to decide if he is with us or against us. And so will you."

Ilse's eyes showed even greater shock, and her lip began to quiver. She behaved as if the man who stood before her was a complete stranger, perhaps one who might even cause her harm. Before the moment could deteriorate any further, General Schmidt approached. "And pray tell, who is this enchantingly lovely woman?" he inquired with exaggerated, theatrical chivalry.

"Hello, General Schmidt," Ilse responded, her voice as gray as her hair.

"It's a perfect day, is it not?" Either he had chosen to ignore her visible anxiety, or his political instincts had kicked in, with the intent to defuse it.

"Yes, it is."

"I have some very good news for the young couple. A house has become available in Herbertstraße."

Annelise gasped as her eyes suddenly lit up like a Christmas tree. "Is it the one with the blue trim?!"

"Hm . . . blue trim. Do you know, I can't recall."

Annelise laughed giddily, and grabbed his elbow, bouncing on her toes with surprising agility for a woman in high heels. She suddenly appeared to revert to the mindset of an eight-year-old girl being tantalized with the promise of a new pet. "Father, please! Tell me! Is it?"

The general smiled, his playful resolve visibly melting in the irresistible glare of his daughter's doe eyes.

"It is," he relented.

Annelise screamed with joy, so loudly that several of the reception guests turned their heads, startled, to make sure everything was all right. "Ohhhh thank you, thank you, thank you!" she shrieked, throwing her arms around him. He laughed with paternal delight as he lifted her off the ground, her legs kicking wildly in the air. Almost immediately, she leapt from his embrace and turned her spirited attention to Ilse. "Frau Vogel, wait until you see this house! It's a dream!"

Ilse, however, appeared unmoved by the munificence of the general's offer. "Herbertstraße. A beautiful neighborhood to be sure. There are many fine homes there. But . . . how will you afford it?" she said, directing this last inquiry to her son.

"It will be no trouble," the general assured her. "The owner has been . . . shall we say, motivated to sell." He tossed a wry, half-cocked smile at Otto and Heinz, who returned it in kind. Otto was certain this home would prove to be quite splendid indeed.

"I see," said Ilse, quietly.

Annelise did not seem to notice her mother-in-law's muted reaction. "Oh, I'm going to throw the most divine parties!" she declared as she planted an ecstatic kiss on her new husband's lips. Otto felt good. Not just from the kiss, but all of it. He began to realize just how truly blessed a life he was destined to lead.

"General Schmidt," said Ilse, fixing a critical eye on the SS man. "Is the owner . . . a Jew?"

Otto was abruptly jolted from his reverie, realizing with horror just how far his mother intended to take this misguided line of inquiry.

"Mama, don't—"

"It's a simple question, Otto," she interrupted, silencing him frostily. She continued, turning back to the general. "Is this man choosing to sell of his own free will? Or is there some other reason?"

"I'm not sure I follow you." The general smiled, seemingly unbothered.

Ilse ceased mincing her words. "Do the new laws compel him to do so? Is that what you mean by . . . motivated to sell, Herr General?"

"Well, Madam, the new restrictions are only temporary," he assured her. "I can promise you, the Führer wants what is best for the country as a whole."

"And . . . does he want what is best for this Jew?"

"He did not say it was a Jew!" Otto snapped at her. This was quite enough. How dare she humiliate him in front of a man as highly respected as General Schmidt. And on his wedding day, no less! He would not stand for it any longer. "Heinz," he said, his stony glare still fixed on his mother, "perhaps you would be so kind as to take my mother outside to see the gardens. They really are quite breathtaking at this time of year."

"Of course, it would be my pleasure," answered Heinz, offering Ilse an arm. She ignored it.

"No need. I can find my own way." And with that, she turned on her heel and strode away, leaving Otto with a mixture of immense relief and profound sadness.

"My sincerest apologies, sir," he said, offering the general a deferential bow of his head. "I'm quite sure my mother is not feeling well. She has been . . . ill, you see."

"No need for apologies, my son." The general grinned warmly, clapping a reassuring hand on the younger man's shoulder. "Change is exciting for some people. Others take a little longer to get used to progress."

"You're . . . very understanding, sir. Thank you."

Moving on as if no unpleasant discourse had occurred, he proffered his elbow. "Come, Annelise. I have not yet danced with my daughter." He winked at Otto. "I promise I will not steal her away from you." As they moved nimbly out onto the dance floor, Annelise craned her neck back over her shoulder and blew Otto a kiss. The band played a lively rendition of Strauss's "Tales from the Vienna Woods" as they spun gaily in celebration of a new phase of life.

CHAPTER FOUR

The jeep pulled up in front of the clockmaker's shop, and Otto stepped out, straightening his coat with a tug, and briefly glancing down once again at the new insignia with pride. Untersturmführer. He had come a long way. The two officers under his command fell into position behind him, awaiting the signal. Heller and Ritter were good men. Reliable. You could count on them in a tight situation. Not that this would be anything of the sort. Otto had a brief flashback to his boyhood, when he had been overpowered by two larger boys right on this very spot. And as if the harassment hadn't been emasculating enough, the old Jew had compounded the humiliation by attempting to come to his rescue. He supposed perhaps he should be civil with Hirschbock. After all, the bastard had only been trying to help him. However, any sense at all that he was obliged to be lenient had long since been smothered by the old man's

obstinance. The regularizing of the restrictions was something Hirschbock would have to accept. It was against the law
for Jewish citizens to own businesses. *And anyway*, thought
Otto, *what do I care what happens to him? He's a stinking, pa-
thetic Jew.* Otto was on his way up, and he did not need the
bother of this one stubborn holdout wasting his time, and
keeping him from more pressing duties.

Otto pushed on the door. It was locked. He stepped
aside and gestured to Heller, who gave it a hard push with
his shoulder. It did not even take his full weight. The door
opened with a loud *crack* of splintered wood.

The three SS entered the shop. Beautiful, ornate clocks
of all shapes and sizes adorned the walls, and the smell of
polished wood filled Otto's nostrils. Behind the counter was
Herr Hirschbock, a magnifying eyepiece inserted in his right
socket as he expertly reconstructed a valuable-looking gold
wristwatch. Startled, he looked up. The eyepiece fell from his
socket, clattering loudly on the table. Hirschbock made no
move to inspect the lens for damage. He stared, unmoving, at
the SS. "We're closed," he said with a frail voice. Otto ignored
this and casually approached the old man without hostility,
knowing full well the machine gun slung from his shoulder
and those of his men would ensure silent intimidation.

"No, you're not," said Otto. "You're open. That's the trouble, hm?"

The old Jew took a step backward. He was scared. Good.
Perhaps this could be done cleanly. "You have received

several notices, Herr Hirschbock. And yet still . . ." Otto gestured dramatically at the array of clocks that surrounded them on all sides.

"I have done nothing wrong!" Hirschbock answered with a tiresome whine. "I have not bothered anyone. Just let me be, please! This establishment has been in my family for generations. It's my life!"

"All the more reason to protect it."

Hirschbock's pleading expression turned bitter. "By giving it up to the *Reich*?" Then, just as abruptly, he appeared docile once more. He looked to Otto with desperate eyes. "Otto Vogel. I remember when you were just a child. You were accosted by two older boys right outside my shop. They robbed you. Pushed you to the ground. I helped you. Help *me. Please.*"

"But that's exactly what I'm trying to do." Otto smiled calmly. Inside, however, he was losing patience. Lunchtime was approaching, and he was getting hungry. "Bitte," he said sharply. "Walk out that door while your skull is still intact."

"Please," the old Jew implored. His hands were now visibly shaking. *A fine watch repairman,* Otto thought with amusement. He nodded to his men. With the usual expressions of delight, Heller and Ritter began smashing the clocks with the butts of their weapons.

"NO! STOP! PLEASE, STOP IT! NO!" The decrepit fool shrieked hysterically as the two SS continued to trash the shop. Evidently having had his fill of manual destruction, Ritter turned his machine gun around and opened fire.

Bullets sprayed the wall, accelerating the damage to the merchandise. *"STOP! I BEG YOU! PLEASE, NO!"*

Otto contemplated taking a few shots himself, just for fun, but then thought better of it. The Führer's genius was that he had conquered so many territories without firing a shot. A shrewd example to follow. Besides, ammunition was costly. Not to mention, the more valuables that were saved, the more that could be absorbed by the Reich. Perhaps one of these clocks would be of interest to Reichsmarschall Göring for his much-admired collection of objets d'art.

Hirschbock was still screaming, and tears were now visible. He was crying. Then, without warning, and for God only knew what reason, he ran directly at Heller, charging like a mad bull. Heller spun on his heel and swiftly and easily clocked the clock-maker with the butt of his weapon. The old Jew collapsed to the floor, bloodied and unconscious. Ritter blasted two cuckoo clocks, and was aiming for a third, when Otto shouted:

"AUFHÖREN!"

There was no need for any more. The man had been dealt with.

"Put him in the truck." The two SS men did as they were told, dragging Hirschbock out by his legs. The Jew's head left a trail of blood that smeared a long, uneven line across the floor of the shop. With a last glance at the ruined establishment, Otto departed. He was looking forward to lunch.

— ✧ —

"You watch," said Heinz, wiping a cumulus cloud of beer foam from his upper lip. "If Hitler decides to march on Poland, it will be another Munich. The English and the French will do anything to avoid a fight. Hitler's the only one with any spine. You watch. You'll see."

There was no debate between the two men. Otto knew Heinz was most likely correct. However, tonight, as he drained mug after mug of dark beer with his friend, enjoying the dim, smoky atmosphere of the crowded pub, his mind was not on war, or conquest, or the expansion of German influence. He was preoccupied with other matters.

"Heinz," he said with a grin, "I have bigger news than a march on Poland."

"Bigger news? Well, this I would like to hear. What is it?"

A nearby table of foreigners erupted in bellowing laughter for the umpteenth time. They were an obnoxious lot, and Otto had to raise his voice over the din.

"Annelise and I." He paused for dramatic effect. "We're going to have a baby."

The look of genuine joy and delight on Heinz's face told Otto, as if he did not already know, that he had a true friend in this man. "Otto!" he said, with a warm clasp of shoulders. "This is fantastic news!"

"Thank you." Otto smiled. "And guess what? She's already designing the nursery. You'd think the baby was coming tomorrow!"

They shared a laugh. "Well, time moves quickly. You'll

be a father before you know it. Otto, congratulations! Let's have a drink on it!" He slapped the bar to attract the bartender's attention. When the mugs arrived, they raised them high. "To the new Vogel!" declared Heinz. "And to a long, prosperous—" He was interrupted once again by the raucous conversation from the table of foreigners, which seemed to crescendo every twenty seconds or so, like waves hitting a beach at high tide, only much more irritating. From the sound of it, there were two British and one American.

"Well, there is a silver lining to all of it," said the first British man. "The Nazis will certainly keep the Communists in check."

The second British man chimed in, every p and b accompanied by a spray of spittle. "Maybe, maybe not. At the moment, it's all speculation. Hitler keeps the entire world guessing, all the time. He's utterly unpredictable. You never know what he's going to say or do next, that's his genius."

"Military geniuses are unpredictable," said the American, puffing on a fat cigar as he slouched back in his chair. "But so are madmen. If you can't tell the difference, you're playing Russian roulette."

"My wife can't stomach the aesthetics of the whole thing," said the first British man. "The gaudy dress, the vulgar pageantry. It's rather astonishing that the Germans are lapping it up the way they are."

"Bunch of suckers and fools, every last one."

By this point, Otto had approached the table. "If you have such a low opinion of Germany, sir, perhaps you should return to America."

The American man shifted his considerable body weight around to see from where the remark had originated. When he saw Otto, smiling coolly in his SS uniform, the American's mouth spread wide with a sneering grin, exposing tobacco-stained, yellowing teeth.

"Well, well! Speak of the devils!" he cackled. "We got a live one right here!" The American's right arm shot upward in a mocking imitation of the traditional Nazi salute. *"Heil Heetlah!"* he hollered, in a poor excuse for a German accent.

"Heil Hitler," Otto responded, offering the same salute with reverential sincerity. "Look around you, sir. Germany has captured the attention of the world thanks to the Führer. Perhaps you should ask the Austrians and the Czechs if we are . . . suckers."

The second British man piped up. "Hitler's leadership skills are undeniable, clearly. But to follow a man simply because he's strong is a risky endeavor."

"Listen, kid," said the American man in his coarse, rhoticity-laden dialect. "Lemme give you a little wake-up call: Hitler's a mobster. You understand? You people are all eating up his propaganda while he goes on a goddamn power trip at your expense. Him and his mobster buddies."

"Ease up, my friend," said the first British man, placing a gentle hand on the American's forearm. He offered Otto an apologetic glance. "He's had perhaps one more beer than he should have."

But Otto kept his attention squarely fixed on the American. It was invariably the Americans who never knew when to quit pompously opining on subjects they knew nothing about. *One day,* Otto silently mused, *Germany's empire under Hitler could very well stretch to the Earth's curve in every direction.* He wished he could look forward in time to witness just how arrogant the Americans would be *then.*

"Even if what you say were so," he explained icily, "you have only yourselves and your English friends to blame. You and your bloodsucking treaty. Hitler is our answer to your shortsightedness, and to your cruelty."

The second British man gave his fellow countryman a gentle shrug. "Well, he's got us there, William. The Versailles treaty was nothing if not shortsighted, in retrospect."

As if counterweighting the Brit's concession, the American turned even surlier. "Maybe you should've stayed inside your own borders in the first place. 'Course, that seems to be a problem for you guys, doesn't it?"

"Borders are drawn by the mighty," said Otto. "The National Socialist Party—"

"*They* may fancy themselves mighty, kid, but either way, *you're* not. Don't delude yourself that this is socialism. What the Soviets have got is socialism. All the Germans did was put a bunch of thugs in the big chairs so they can live like kings while everyone else gets squat. And if you have the balls to ask for your share, you wind up in the camps. Right there with the Jews."

Otto bristled. Again with the goddamn Jews. You would think the bloody democracies worshiped these people as deities. "The Jews are being treated fairly," he assured the old blowhard.

"Oh yeah? I've seen a few torched synagogues that tell a different story."

"Our response has been measured. The restrictions are entirely appropriate."

The American man snorted. "I'll be damned if I know why the French didn't just slap Hitler down after he occupied the Rhineland."

"Because they're the French," snarked the first British man. "Why get your hands dirty when you could be feasting on chocolates and women? Honestly, I'm rather surprised they haven't rolled over themselves."

"Indeed, every conqueror finds his shortest route through Paris, eh?" remarked the second British man. They both chuckled, as if reveling in their cleverness.

"Just so," said Otto.

The American man drained the last of his beer in one gulp. "Take my advice, kid. The Nazis are a cult of psychopaths. And their leader is a goon who fifteen years ago couldn't even get a job shoveling horse manure."

Clearly this drunken fool wasn't getting the message. A more direct educational tactic was called for. Otto grabbed the man by the collar, and took a hard swing. The blow landed with a sickening thwack, and the American tumbled backward out of his chair, a hilarious bug-eyed expression on his sweaty face. That should have done the trick, but libation had partially numbed his ability to feel pain, and had, conversely, fortified his courage. He stumbled to his feet and half lunged, half fell toward Otto. As Otto moved to push him away, the American landed two jabs to Otto's midsection. Either he was pathetically weak by nature or too inebriated to focus his thrust, because the impact was negligible. Otto had to laugh aloud. By the time Heinz rushed over to help his friend, the American was facedown on the floor, unconscious. The scuffle was over.

Otto did not notice the angular, salt-and-pepper-haired man watching from the bar.

Two days later, Otto read the headline: HITLER AND STALIN SIGN PACT OF NON-AGGRESSION. Germany and Russia were to be allies. Hitler had once again pulled off a masterful feat. He had utterly duped the British into the belief that he was truly negotiating with them. *Well,* thought Otto, *either this means a triumphant next stage of German expansion . . . or there may be war after all.*

CHAPTER FIVE

Otto ran a finger gently down the bladelike edge of the crease in his trousers, and silently thanked Annelise for taking such good care of him. She knew as well as he did that for whatever purpose he had been summoned to this meeting, immaculate dress would be essential. Whether he would be accepting praise or pleading for forgiveness, he had no idea. He knew only that the Hauptsturmführer had sent for him. The reason was a mystery.

"Untersturmführer Vogel," said the adjutant in an efficient, clipped voice as he appeared in the doorway, "the Hauptsturmführer will see you now."

Otto rose obediently, and followed the expressionless man into a dark, wood-paneled office that smelled pleasantly of pipe tobacco. Expensive-looking leather chairs bookended a couch, before which a wooden coffee table displayed a small, metallic sculpture of a wolf. The expected oversized portrait of the Führer hung on the opposite wall, beneath which a bespectacled man with ruddy cheeks and a receding hairline sat at a large oak desk, working his way through a stack of paperwork with rigid intensity. The adjutant abruptly left the room without a word, and there was a terribly awkward moment during which Otto was unsure whether he should announce himself, and in fact wondered if the dour-looking man was even aware that he was in the room. At last, however, the man looked up, and uttered a bland, bureaucratic "Heil Hitler."

"Heil Hitler!" Otto responded with ten times the passion, his right arm launching itself into the air reflexively.

"Please sit down, Untersturmführer." He gestured to a stained and polished wooden chair adjacent to the desk. Otto sat dutifully and waited for whatever was to come next.

The Hauptsturmführer riffled through his pile of papers, and extracted a folder. He began skimming the pages inside. Either he had an enviably impressive poker face, or he was simply bored. Otto couldn't tell which.

"I've received many favorable reports from your superiors," he said. "It seems your service record is quite exemplary." Otto breathed a mental sigh of relief. It appeared this was going to go well.

"Thank you, sir," he responded, careful to keep his tone restrained and non-indicative of the inward delight he was feeling.

"We were particularly impressed with your handling of the American."

"The . . . American?" Otto was confused.

"At the pub. Some months ago. You were observed with great interest. Your allegiance is commendable."

"Thank you, sir." Now he recalled. The drunken American he had roughed up. Good God, the Nazis really did have eyes everywhere.

The Hauptsturmführer closed his folder, and for the first time he looked Otto directly in the eyes. "There is a consensus . . . that a new posting would be appropriate at this time. We feel you would make a fine Obersturmführer."

Otto's heartbeat accelerated. A promotion!

"Does that sound . . . appealing?" The Hauptsturmführer leaned back in his chair.

"Very much so, sir. Yes," Otto answered, again carefully modulating his tone.

"Good. You are aware of . . . certain measures being taken to contend with . . . the Jewish problem?"

"I am, yes."

"I can tell you that our success in Poland is only the beginning. There is still much work to do. Germany needs loyal men of . . . discretion. Would you describe yourself as such a man, Herr Vogel? A man of . . . discretion?"

Otto stiffened with assuredness. "I serve the Führer," he said with genuine pride.

The dour man actually cracked a smile.

—— ✧ ——

It's so remarkably flat. That was Otto's initial impression of the Polish countryside. Flat, flat, and more flat. Now he realized why the campaign had been so successful, and so swift. *It's practically designed to be invaded.* He worried that Annelise would be bored here. After all, she was accustomed to such a glamorous, kinetic lifestyle, having spent so much of her youth at the white-hot center of Berlin's high society. As he watched her cradling their beautiful new baby boy, Alger, however, he knew his fears were unwarranted. She was deeply loyal, and she knew what she had signed up for. If he was the tree, she was as tight as the bark.

He stared out the window at the passing landscape, allowing the train's gentle movements to partially tranquilize him. He observed the shattered husk of an old stone church, no doubt obliterated by the precise targeting skill of the Luftwaffe. It had probably stood there for centuries. "It's a shame they put up a fight," he said regretfully. "We could have preserved more."

"Alger is so quiet," Annelise whispered. "The motion soothes him."

"I know how he feels. I could fall asleep right now." But he kept his eyes open. And smiled at her.

"What's that for?" she asked.

"Because you look so beautiful."

Suddenly wide-awake, he realized that the train's vibrations coupled with the presence of Annelise fetchingly dolled-up for travel had stirred in him an unexpected arousal. He moved across to the other side of the compartment and kissed her passionately. She giggled with pleasure, and urged through occupied lips, "Be careful! Don't wake him." But her resistance was superficial. Otto tingled as her gentle hand moved along his arm and up to his face, her fingers like flower petals on his body.

"Annelise, this is only the beginning for us," he vowed softly, taking her hands in his. "With the war going as well as it is, a German victory is only a matter of time. When Europe is normalized again, you will be a queen among peasants. I promise it."

"I love you, Otto Vogel." She kissed him back as Alger slept peacefully, her cheeks glowing red with desire.

CHAPTER SIX

His cheeks flared red with belligerence.

"The rules here are simple! Work hard, and you will be fed. You will have a place to sleep. And you will be treated well. Certainly much better than you deserve." The pathetic-looking gaggle of Jews avoided eye contact, either looking down at the dirt or staring ahead with glassy eyes, their intracranial workings as inscrutable as they were irrelevant. Otto sized them up with disgust. It was astounding that Germany had once allowed these creatures to share their elevated civilization, to dine in the same restaurants, to absorb the same culture, the same art, the same symphonies, as if the mind of the Jew had any real capacity to process these things beyond the context of its own self-interest. The sooner Europe was rid of this unsavory blight, the better. And not just Europe. The world.

The newly transported bunch appeared docile enough,

standing rigidly in formation, looking like a row of stalag-mites enveloped in deteriorating, imperiled flesh. It was doubtful any of them would cause trouble. As always, however, there was nothing to lose by an early display of authority. And it could save some headaches down the line.

"I have no doubt that most of you will comply without incident," Otto continued, moving at a leisurely pace down the row of haggard, indistinguishable faces. "However, there are always one or two agitators who seek to make trouble for the rest." He moved closer to the lineup, scanning each pair of eyes with a formidable glare. This was pure theatrics. He hadn't really bothered to study individual features, at least not since he'd first taken command of the camp. It wasn't worth it, as enough of them would be liquidated by tomor-row, soon replaced by still more who would be liquidated in equally short order. It was only the strong and the hardy who warranted prolonging the inevitable, at least as long as they could be useful workers. Strong and hardy, however, were rare features when it came to Jews.

"Who will it be, hm? Who amongst you will disrupt the orderly operation of this camp?" No answer, as usual. "Oh, come now. I've seen thousands of you miserable Jews come and go. There's always a bad apple. Always. So, what do we do, eh? We could wait and see who it might be. But that would be inefficient. Efficiency! Yes! That is the lifeblood of a thriving work camp! So. Let us not wait. Let us find out right now."

He strolled back down the row of shivering, twitching

prisoners. God, they stank, even in this cold wind. The fresh meat is not so fresh. He stopped in front of a gaunt, gray-scruffed old Jew who looked to be around sixty. Hardly a likely candidate for heavy work. He would not be missed.

"You! Jew! Step forward!"

The prisoner stared at Otto, his face frozen in a stupid, wide-eyed expression.

"JETZT! SCHNELL!"

Two of the guards cocked their rifles. Good men. They knew when to take their cue. At last, the shriveled old prune shakily stepped forward. Otto offered a smile, which stretched into a grin.

"Guten Tag," he said.

The Jew did not answer.

"I said Guten Tag," he repeated, with firm impatience.

"Gute . . . guten Tag," the Jew responded, his voice a frail whisper.

"Are you having a good day?"

"Y-yes, sir."

"Do you like it here?"

"Yes, sir."

Otto threw his head back, emitting a harsh belly laugh. "Are you blind and stupid, Jew? You're a prisoner in a bloody labor camp! How could you possibly like it here? How dare you lie to me!" It looked for a moment as if the Jew might speak, but it was just the chattering of his teeth in the bitter wind, no doubt amplified by fear. "I ask again,"

Otto snapped, "Do you like it here?"

"No. No, sir."

"No, of course not. You hate it. You wish you could be anywhere else. And you hate me, don't you? Be truthful, now."

"Yes, sir."

"Yes, you do. You hate me because I am your master. You think I'm a son of a bitch. Tell me so."

The Jew feebly extended his open palms in a gesture of supplication. "Please, I—"

"Tell me," Otto ordered, ignoring the entreaty. "Say 'You're a son of a bitch,' unless you want those men to shoot you where you stand." The Jew tossed a momentary glance at the scowling guards, then managed to croak out his response.

"You're . . . a . . . son of a . . . bitch."

Otto laughed again, harder this time, and was joined by the guards. He felt a sudden odd but welcome sensation of pride in being German, and a feeling of esprit de corps as he watched his men enjoying the show. "Ohohoho! Well, look at that!" he cackled. "I think we've found our troublemaker!"

The Jew's knees quavered, and he looked as if he might vomit. Otto advanced until he was an inch from the man's nose. "Run," he whispered.

"No, I—I ca—"

"RUN!!"

His eyes wild with animal terror, the shocked Jew half stumbled, half scurried out into the expanse of the main

yard, at first zigzagging like a panicked rabbit, and then darting toward the nearest edge of the fenced enclosure. Otto
and the guards watched the spastic, striped figure stagger
away as fast as he was evidently able. This was the part that
made the admittedly overwrought preamble worthwhile. It
was like a game. Otto drew his pistol, and fired. Direct hit!
The body collapsed into the dirt, a neat, clean hole in the
back of the skull. The guards shouted their approval and all
appropriate congratulations.

"There." Otto smiled triumphantly, turning back to face
the rest of the prisoners. "Now that the riffraff is gone, we
have an obedient, well-behaved bunch, yes? Good! So, to
work!"

The Jews just stared in dumbfounded horror at the crumpled remains. One of them was involuntarily urinating. Otto
fired his pistol into the air.

"TO WORK!!"

They all scattered in random directions, each grasp-
ing for the nearest shovel, pickaxe, or other implement to
avoid being the next to receive a fatal injection of lead. As
it occurred to Otto that he very much felt like a cigarette,
an Untersturmführer whose name he could not remember
approached with a folded slip of paper.

"Kommandant," the man said, "a message for you. From
the office of Reichsführer Himmler."

Otto felt his stomach lurch, and the ground beneath his
feet seemed to sway as if he was on the deck of a sailing ship.

Himmler!

The shock was such that the message may as well have come from Adolf Hitler himself. Otto snatched the telegram from the subordinate, feeling a volatile mixture of excitement and panic not unlike his first visit to the Hauptsturmführer, where he had received the thrilling news of this very posting.

He opened it, and read.

If his stomach had lurched before, it now felt as if it were attempting a twisting armstand dive. Despite the cold of the raw morning, he instantly began to sweat as he read:

> *Two selected representatives from the International Committee of the Red Cross will be arriving in ten days to tour and inspect the facility, as approved by the office of the Reichsführer. Please make all appropriate preparations and arrangements.*

Otto gaped dumbly at the printed letters. He whirled to face the Untersturmführer, fixing him with a glare that demanded answers. "The Red Cross?! Here? Has he gone completely mad?!" The Untersturmführer, of course, was merely the messenger, and hardly equipped to shed light.

"I don't know, Herr Kommandant. They have been granted limited access to Theresienstadt, so perhaps—"

"THIS IS NOT THERESIENSTADT!"

The other officer cut short his speculation. "Yes, Herr Kommandant."

"Sheiße," muttered Otto. Accessibility meant vulnerability. He knew the Reich had an interest in projecting an outward image of humane treatment when it came to the Jews, which was why they had permitted a rare inspection tour by members of the International Red Cross at Theresienstadt. However, that was largely a transit site, where the pretense of decency was easier to maintain. Most of its prisoners were dispatched to their deaths in other camps, which meant that there were no liquidation facilities to conceal. But perhaps, with every prisoner working round the clock ...

"Very well. Send a response. Tell the office of the Reichsführer to rest assured we will be more than prepared."

"Yes, Kommandant."

It was time to show these wretched Jews what hard work really was.

The car pulled into the roundabout driveway of the stately Kommandant's residence. Otto admired the clean, hard lines of the stonework, and the sleek high windows above the main entryway. Annelise had initially found the structure cold and forbidding, but he had given her wide creative latitude to transform the interior to better suit her tastes. The result was a warm, plush, inviting atmosphere adorned with fresh flowers daily, and a myriad of sweet smells that advertised the gustatory delights awaiting him each evening. Annelise had taken instantly to the role of housemistress, efficiently guiding the work of the servants from maids to cooks, and she had masterfully created a sort of cocoon that Otto was grateful to come home to after the gnawing cold of the camp.

He idly tugged at the waist of his trousers. He had put on a bit of weight since turning thirty. He would have to have the seamstress let out his pants a bit. As the driver slowed the car to a stop, Otto noticed another vehicle parked in the driveway. He hurried to the large, wooden front door, which opened even before he reached it. Though his mind was racing, he was still able to take a split second to appreciate his wife's beauty. She was dressed in an elegant, deep-blue ensemble with white fringe about the shoulders, sleeves, and waist, an expression of sparkling readiness on her face as she held Alger in her arms.

"Va-ta!" said Alger. His words were getting better and better every day. Otto gave both wife and son a quick peck on the cheek, and glanced past her shoulder into the foyer.

"Are they here?" he asked anxiously.

"Yes, darling. They're in the parlor. I had Olga serve the tea and cakes. They seem relaxed and satisfied."

"All right. Let's get this over with."

He strode into the parlor, removing his hat with a deferential nod of the head, showing a respect he did not feel. This highly invasive formal probe, after all, was proving to be a gigantic headache.

There were two of them: a man and a woman. She was tall, with brownish-blonde hair done up in a neat, tight bun. She was quite attractive, but with a clear air of authority, unmistakable despite the disarming smile she gave him. The man was dark-haired, brown-eyed, and genteel in his demeanor, as in the manner of a politician. Both were poised and well-dressed. All in all, they were not what he expected from representatives of the International Red Cross.

"Kommandant Vogel," said the man in surprisingly impeccable German, extending a hand.

Otto took it gamely. "Yes. Welcome."

"I'm Ed Mercer. And this is my associate, Kelly Grayson."

CHAPTER SEVEN

A dozen or so Jews had died from overwork in the process, but they had quickly been replaced, and the results were astounding. The camp had been more than adequately transformed in time for the inspection. The barracks had been painted and trimmed, colorful flower beds had been planted, and the healthiest of the prisoners were now strolling about, clothed in clean, weather-appropriate, presentable attire. The women's dresses were pretty enough even by outside standards, and some of the men even wore hats. Young children could be seen running about, playing a game of tag near a small playground area complete with a see-saw and a wooden slide. There was no trace of the weedy, undernourished prisoners who normally inhabited the camp. Some had been relocated, others had been liquidated. Otto guided Mercer and Grayson through the grounds of the facility with pride and satisfaction.

"As you can see," he assured them, "our Jewish occupants are being well treated and provided for. They are more than adequately nourished, they have access to soap and clean water, and we even have our own laundry."

Mercer nodded, apparently contented with what he saw. "Very encouraging," he agreed.

This was going better and more smoothly than expected. Otto pressed on. "Once every two weeks, we screen a film in the barracks, and on Sunday nights, the cooks prepare cakes and pies— Ah! *This* is something to see. Look there. Some of our younger residents have become curious about the American sport of baseball. I think they're quite good, yes?" As they approached the game, Otto privately fumed as he noticed the expressions on the children's faces. They were dead-eyed, lifeless. Where were the smiles he had demanded under threat of punishment? Where was the laughter? They had been given a week's worth of regular meals in preparation for this day! If these little Jew brats exposed him and this operation, he would personally see them liquidated before lunchtime, Red Cross be damned. He guided Mercer and Grayson toward the other end of the grounds. "Now, if you'll follow me, I'll show you the inside of the barracks. You will find the accommodations to be more than—"

"Please! Help us! They're killing us!"

Otto stopped dead in his tracks, and felt a wave of combined panic and rage as he turned around. One of the prisoners had broken away from his assigned facade, and was staggering toward Mercer and Grayson. Otto nodded sharply to the nearest guard, who approached the disruptive Jew, a short-ish, balding creature of about forty, as Otto hastily began damage control.

"My apologies," he said, mustering a reassuring smile for the visitors. "Micha has had some psychological difficulties—"

"This!" the Jew shouted with wild eyes. *"This is all a lie! They're killing us!"*

"I assure you, he's getting the very best medical care that we can provide for him," said Otto.

The guard had begun gently but firmly to pull the upstart away from the scene. *"Please! Help! I beg you! Help us!"* The guard pulled harder.

"NO!"

With remarkable adrenaline-fueled speed, the Jew violently struck the guard square in the face. Utterly unprepared for—and unused to—this level of rebellion, the guard was momentarily stunned. But one moment was enough. The prisoner wrested the guard's machine gun free, and turned it on him. He fired, spraying a load of bullets directly into the guard's chest. The man was dead instantly.

Within seconds, every other weapon within the perimeter was at the ready, trained on the prisoner. All across the grounds, the newly groomed Jews froze, stunned by what was happening. The guards cocked their guns.

"No! Wait!" shouted Otto. Perhaps this situation could still be salvaged from a political standpoint. If not . . . if the Red Cross's report was not what it must be . . . well, the thought of failing Reichsführer Himmler was too unthinkable to contemplate. The consequences would very likely cost him his career . . . and possibly more than that.

Otto slowly and cautiously moved toward the prisoner. "Micha," he said in the gentlest tone of which he was capable, "put down the weapon. We want to help you."

Micha stared with a crazed look in his eye, but did not yet shoot. His hand shook. It's the first time he's ever killed a man, thought Otto. He's reeling. He's still processing it. Otto took advantage of the moment. "No one is going to hurt you. I promise." He moved closer. Closer. If that goddamned Jew with his quivering hand accidentally pulled the trigger . . .

Otto moved closer. He put a hand on his sidearm.

The prisoner fired.

Otto was hit.

The bullets passed right through him.

He looked down at his own body.

Nothing. No wounds. No blood.

Not even a scratch or a graze.

Was it possible . . . ?

Could every single bullet have missed its mark?

At point-blank range?

The Jew rushed toward Otto and fired again.

And again, the bullets passed through him, as if they were spirits of the deceased. He did not even feel a change in air pressure. He was completely unharmed.

It was inconceivable that anyone could have missed at that range with that weapon.

One of the other guards then opened fire, shooting the prisoner in the head. He fell to the ground, unmoving.

Otto was in shock. He stared blankly at the other guards, who appeared equally dumbfounded.

"It's . . . impossible," one of them whispered softly with awe.

Mercer stepped forward. "Herr Vogel," he said. "We can explain what's happening."

Even through his shock, Otto slowly became aware of a peculiarity: The two Red Cross representatives appeared utterly unmoved or undisturbed by the miraculous event that had just occurred. The astonishment that was evident on the faces of everyone else present was absent from these two.

Grayson spoke the first of many words that would shatter Otto's world forever.

"Hold simulation."

It happened instantaneously. The guards, the prisoners, everyone . . . froze where they were. The cold was gone. The wind was gone. All was silent. Otto looked to his left, where an armed guard stood motionless, in mid-stride. One foot was off the ground, with a small cloud of dust in its wake. The dust did not move.

"What . . . what trick is this?" he hissed furiously, though in the sound of his own voice he heard far more fear than rage. He marched straight at the frozen guard, moving to grab the man by the shoulders. "Answer me NOW!"

He passed right through him.

Otto fell to the ground, landing hard on his face. Of course there was no pain. There never was. Never had been.

He awkwardly turned himself over and looked up. In the sky above him, a wood pigeon hung in place, its wings spread in mid-flight. But it did not move. Otto felt as if he were oozing out of his own body, watching events unfold from a detached place. Is this what it's like to go mad . . . ?

As if in a dream, Mercer and Grayson approached him. He became freshly aware of a small brown satchel that hung from Grayson's shoulder. The guard at the gate had inspected it upon entry, but all was in order. Now she removed it, reached in, and pulled out what appeared to be a white robe of some kind.

"Herr Vogel," she said, "please put this on."

"Wh-what . . . ?" He felt disoriented, nauseous, ready to vomit.

"Please, put this on over your uniform. And we'll tell you what's going on."

Mercer gave him what was clearly intended to be a reassuring look. "Trust us," he said.

With no other apparent move presenting itself, Otto extended a quivering hand, and took the robe. It was soft. Impossibly soft. The threads of the fabric were finer than the most expensive garment he had ever seen or felt. He put on the robe. Mercer helped Otto to his feet, though it was unclear whether his legs would continue to operate under their own power.

"Herr Vogel . . . Otto," said Mercer, "I'm going to tell you something that will be very hard for you to believe. But you're going to have to try."

"What . . . ?"

"Your world . . . is not real."

The man was speaking nonsense. Otto neither believed nor disbelieved what was being said, because it was the statement of a drunk, or a dope user. Wait . . . was that it? Had he somehow been drugged? Of course! Now it made sense. He was under the influence of a narcotic. But why? And how?

Mercer continued. "What is about to happen is going to be extremely traumatizing. But you need to know that you are safe. No one here is going to harm you."

Deceptively palliative words no doubt oft uttered by torturers before a brutal interrogation.

"Who are you?" Otto demanded.

Mercer and Grayson exchanged a glance that seemed to silently communicate some moment of decisiveness.

"End simulation," said Grayson.

And Otto's world disintegrated.

CHAPTER EIGHT

Ed and Kelly had prepared for this moment under the guidance of a specially selected team of Union psychiatric authorities, but now, when presented with the reality, it was hard not to feel a little helpless. As the artificial environment of the concentration camp pixelated itself out of existence, leaving only the bare, silver-toned interior of the environmental simulator, they witnessed something akin to a nonhuman mammal having a petrifying subjective mental experience the emotional particulars of which were impenetrable to any outside observer. The exploitative installations that were once called "zoos" had been abolished for centuries, but seeing the abject animal terror on this man's face in this moment gave Ed and Kelly a taste of what it must have been like to see a tiger trapped in a cage. He wondered how humans had ever been able to suppress their compassion and to derive pleasure from the sight. The unpleasant recollection of the Calivon incident flashed across Ed's mind. He and Kelly knew all too well how it felt to be on the other side of those bars.

Wide-eyed and panicked, Adam darted his gaze about, birdlike, until he became aware of Ed and Kelly cautiously approaching. He scrambled to a corner, his breathing fast and heavy, beads of sweat popping out along his brow. He pulled the robe tighter, obviously aware of his nakedness beneath, his SS uniform now gone along with his world.

"It's all right," Kelly said softly, her hands outstretched in the universal gesture of peace. "You're going to be okay. I know this is scary, but I promise you, everything is going to be okay."

Without warning, Adam lurched forward and vomited onto the floor. To his obvious astonishment, the mess instantly vanished, its molecules efficiently appropriated by the computer.

"Mercer to Finn," Ed said, tapping his comm. "We need you."

The simulator doors opened, and Claire entered, her green field uniform instantly providing a subtle sense of relief to Ed. Claire had requested assignment to the *Orville* because she had felt she could be useful to a new and untried captain with a less than perfect record—that she could be an essential guiding force, as opposed to the nagging ship's doctor that a crew avoided like the plague. At first, Ed had been privately irked by the presumption that he needed an adviser or counselor to help him do his job, but in the past few years, he had come to trust and rely on Claire as no one else. He could not imagine captaining the *Orville* without the ever-present security of her watchful eye.

Adam pressed his shaking form even more tightly against the wall, as if trying to move through it as the simulated bullets had moved through his torso. Claire approached with watchful guardedness, slowly opening her medscanner and taking great care to avoid any sudden moves. She scanned Adam, who seemed both petrified and mesmerized by the little device with its glittering lights and glowing screen.

"He's in shock," Claire said, at last turning to Ed and Kelly. "I wouldn't recommend transporting him in this condition. If he's this traumatized now, the experience of a shuttle flight into space could be more than his mind can handle."

"Well, we can't leave him down here," said Kelly.

"I can sedate him. Of course, we're only prolonging the inevitable."

Ed weighed the options. "All right," he said. He turned back to Adam. "The doctor needs to give you some medicine. It's harmless, I promise." However, Claire had taken less than two steps before Adam frantically scrambled to the other side of the simulator, huddling in the far corner. It was clear this was going to be much more difficult than they had hoped.

"Claire," Ed asked with reluctance, "can he handle a stun?"

"He can. If that's what you think is best."

"His military training is real. I think it'd be easiest."

Distasteful as it was, Claire agreed. Ed nodded to Kelly, who reached into her satchel and extracted her pulser.

"I'm sorry," she said with genuine empathy as she raised the weapon and aimed it at Adam. His eyes widened momentarily, and then the quick, merciful blast rendered him unconscious.

"Okay," said Ed, "let's get him out of here."

As he and Kelly lifted Adam's limp body, Claire noticed something on the floor at the far end of the simulator. Upon closer examination, she found that it was a small pile of clothes. She picked it up.

Baby clothes. A light blue blanket.

Her breath caught as she realized what she was holding.

The clothing in which baby Adam had been swaddled when he had been left here, so many years ago. The simulator had of course preserved the items, and now that the program was deactivated, they were all that remained.

Claire stuffed the clothing into her medical bag, and hurried out.

Ed and Kelly hauled the sleeping Adam down the corridor toward the lift. They passed large glass windows that looked in on the well-equipped but long-abandoned labs, perfectly preserved save for several layers of thick dust. Claire joined them as they reached the lift, and Kelly hit the touch panel. "Surface level."

The lift ascended, and they soon found themselves once again surrounded by the bright, arid expanse of the planet. They carried Adam into the shuttle, strapped him in, and shortly thereafter they were airborne, en route to the orbiting *Orville*, and all the uncertainty that lay ahead.

CHAPTER NINE

The two scientists looked somberly down upon the slumbering figure, a thousand emotions battling for supremacy within their collective psyches. His was the face of a man they had never known. And yet, they were acutely aware of the unsettling reality: He was their son.

Leonard and Pamela Collier were both in their early sixties, trim and gaunt, with the deep lines of time carved into their faces—lines that told the story of hard, traumatic lives. Adam Collier was still unconscious as he lay on the sickbay bed, heavily sedated for the time being. Ed, Kelly, and Claire stood watching, along with Talla, whose ears and forehead were carefully concealed by a wrap in the unlikely event that the patient should awaken before he was revived. Mother and father regarded the cultural anomaly that was their offspring. There was a slight quaver in Pamela's voice as she spoke.

"I've . . . pictured this moment in my mind a billion times over. And I didn't think it would be anything like this. I feel like I'm looking at a complete stranger."

"That's understandable," said Claire, her bedside manner soothing as always.

"We thought we were saving him," said Leonard. "Giving him a chance to survive. My God, he would've been better off in prison with us."

"No, he wouldn't have," Ed assured them. "Look at him. At least he's alive and unharmed. No one could have made the same guarantee if he were in a Krill prison. You did what you could."

Claire approached the couple. "Mr. and Mrs. Collier, how are you feeling? Health-wise?"

"The Union medical corps was amazing," said Pamela, mustering a wan smile. "We felt very looked after."

"And . . . psychologically?"

"Psychologically . . . time will tell. Right now I'm just so grateful that Adam is alive."

"I know this is an emotional time for you," said Kelly, treading lightly, "but if you're willing, we'd like to hear your full report. If you need time to rest, that's all right as well. But we do generally prefer to debrief as early as possible, while information is still fresh in the subject's mind."

"Of course, Commander," said Leonard with a nod. "We can begin right away."

"Thank you. It's appreciated."

Ed turned to his chief of security. "Talla, we'll be in my office. I want a standard security detail on duty here when he wakes up. All human. No offense."

"Understood, sir." For Ed, Talla's tough, hard-edged demeanor had taken some getting used to after the departure of Alara, the *Orville*'s prior security chief, who had returned to her home planet of Xelayah the previous year. It had been sad for the crew, but particularly difficult for Ed, who had developed a substantial trust in Alara, as well as a genuine investment in her well-being. It was peculiar to feel so protective of someone whose very job it was to protect you. However, Talla had proven herself on multiple occasions to be as capable an officer as one could find anywhere in the fleet, and she had pulled the crew out of more than one tough spot. He had grown to like her.

As Talla departed, Ed gestured to Leonard and Pamela. "If you'll follow me."

For a moment, Pamela did not move. Then she silently drew closer to the sickbay bed, and the sleeping form of the thirty-year-old man who somehow was her son. She leaned over and gently kissed his forehead. Ed and Kelly could see the soft glistening of tears in her eyes.

"Friends and colleagues always asked us why we chose to live so far out on the border. Our standard reply was that we enjoyed the peace and solitude. No one questioned it." Leonard's voice was calm and even as he leaned back on the sofa, gently squeezing his wife's hand as he glanced around the soft-toned interior of Ed's office. Perhaps the squeeze was a gesture of pure affection, or perhaps they both needed the moral support. Ed and Kelly sat opposite the Colliers, listening closely to their story.

"You knew that null-space-energy research was illegal," said Kelly, doing her best to keep all traces of judgment from her voice. The regulatory violation was, after all, decades past.

"We knew," answered Pamela, less able than Kelly to conceal her perspective. Shame and deep regret coated her words. "That's why we built the lab underground, and forti-fied it the way we did. By the time we were done, it was invis-ible even to the tightest scans. But, Commander, we honestly believed that the core principles of null-space energy could be used to create a virtually limitless power source."

Kelly's nose wrinkled a bit. "Thousands of researchers before you had failed in that pursuit."

"Not to mention," Ed added, "more than a few died in the process. That . . . must have taken a lot of . . . confidence."

"Arrogance," Leonard corrected him with evident humility. "You can say it. We suspected it even before the attack. It was soul-crushing, but science doesn't lie. So we decided we'd cook the data one last time, and then bury it forever. Visualization is massively helpful to that kind of analysis, which is why we installed the simulator down there. It became an invaluable tool, and as a bonus, it provided recreation during breaks."

"We had run that simulation dozens of times," Pamela said, her eyes growing distant as her mind's eye drifted back into the past. "It was one of my favorites. New York City at the dawn of the twentieth century. April 1914 to be exact. Leonard gave it to me for our first wedding anniversary. We were in the simulator that afternoon. Both Leonard and I had synthesized period attire, so we really felt immersed in that long-ago world. We decided to take Adam with us, so he could experience a piece of history. I mean, not that he really would've been aware of it, he was less than a year old at the time, but he had never actually been to Earth. We were having tea and sandwiches at a sidewalk café when we heard the blasts."

"At first we thought it was part of the simulation," said Leonard. "It was, of course, adaptive like any good program, but still it didn't make sense. The program was set prior to World War One. And it was New York, not Europe. It was then that we realized the blasts were coming from the surface of the planet. We ran to check the security scans, and we were horrified at what we saw. Krill soldiers. A whole contingent of them. We're still not sure how they found us. Most likely it was our supplier. He was a neutral Horbalak named Kiljuk. We didn't really trust him ourselves, but he was reliable with his deliveries. Probably tipped off the Krill for a tidy sum."

"Kiljuk didn't know about the lab, so he couldn't have

exposed its existence," said Pamela, "but it didn't matter. The Krill would've torn the residence to shreds, and they would've found it eventually. So we decided to give them what they wanted, and hope they'd take it and go away." It was a lot tougher now for Ed and Kelly to hide the judgment in their eyes. To voluntarily hand over any viable data concerning null-space-energy research to the Krill was potentially putting millions of lives at risk. Pamela's tone turned slightly defensive.

"I know what you're thinking. But . . . let me ask you this. Do either of you have children?" Ed and Kelly both shifted in their seats. Of course they did not have any children together. It was a complicated and emotional topic. They had discussed it during the time they were married, but their marriage had collapsed before they had gotten any further. To make matters more knotty and textured, Ed had later discovered that he in fact had a daughter with Teleya, the Krill woman who had seduced and exploited him by assuming the identity of a human crew member. However, neither he nor Kelly wanted to bring any of this into the immediate conversation.

"We . . . both understand that the drive to protect one's child is the strongest biological impulse there is," Ed answered, hating the sound of his own voice and the oily political doublespeak he was dishing out. But it was the best he could come up with in the moment. Mercifully, Pamela plowed ahead.

"Exactly," she declared. "Captain, all we cared about was Adam. Whatever happened to us, we had to protect him. So we . . . left him in the care of the simulation. The hotel clerk always seemed like a kindly character, and we could only hope he was programmed with a nurturing instinct. I gave him my baby, and Leonard and I went up to the surface and voluntarily handed all our data over to the Krill."

"It's definitely an . . . unorthodox decision," said Kelly, still processing the insanity of it all, "but I understand why you did what you did."

"We hoped the Krill would count it as a victory and leave us alone, in which case we could go back and get Adam, clear out the lab, and get the hell off the planet," Leonard said, "but acquiring the research wasn't enough for them. They wanted the scientists who developed it. So off they took us, still dressed in that ancient apparel, to their dark homeworld."

"And . . . you never mentioned that you had a child?" Kelly inquired.

"To those fanatics? Of course not! How could we?"

"No, you couldn't. I understand."

Pamela went on. "The lab's main power array was designed to sustain itself for decades if needed. All we could do was hope that someone might find Adam. It was better than giving him to the Krill. But it turned out . . ."—her voice broke for moment—"it turned out we had hidden ourselves too well."

Leonard caressed her hand supportively. "The Krill tried

everything from coercion to torture," he said, "but they wouldn't accept that we hadn't cracked the problem. They were certain we were hiding some vital element. It's the only reason they didn't kill us. They thought we'd eventually break one day. Then, finally, after taking us to hell and back, they decided we were telling the truth."

Despite their criminal activity, Ed now found that he was feeling significant compassion for these people. "And all that time, the Union thought you were dead," he mused. "I'm sure you've heard how completely shocked the admirals were when you were offered up in the prisoner exchange."

Pamela looked down at her husband's hand clasping her own. "We thought about Adam every waking moment of every day. Our beautiful baby boy. We hoped . . ." Her face had become wet with tears. "But then, the time came when hope seemed delusional. As the years went by . . . we forced ourselves to accept that he couldn't have survived."

Leonard leveled a glare of intense disbelief toward Ed and Kelly, as if he were only now fully processing the horrible and bizarre magnitude of what had happened to their son. "With what you've told us," he said, "I'm . . . I'm not sure he did survive." The grim statement hung heavily in the air for a moment. "That simulation was designed for one day . . . one place."

"It was adaptive, though," said Ed.

"Yes. It was. But the fact that the computer extrapolated from the historical files, and expanded the algorithms on its own . . . for over thirty years . . . and turned him into that . . ."

"The computer saved his life," his wife reminded him.

"I know that. I do. But . . . my God, why couldn't it have been France? Or England? Or Dallas, Texas, for that matter? Why did the goddamn program have to pick Germany?"

"Of course the program has no consciousness," Ed said, not sure if he was helping or rubbing salt into the wound. "There was nothing you or anyone could've done to prevent this. The algorithms just . . . threw randomized narrative suggestions at him. When he responded to any particular one, the program would amplify that derivative. It's adaptive interaction. It's nobody's fault."

"It's nobody's fault that that machine turned our son into a killer," Leonard snapped, bitterly. The cynicism in his tone cast an unbroken silence over the room. There was nothing more to say.

CHAPTER TEN

I t was an unusual sight to see a red-uniformed security guard
stationed directly outside Dr. Finn's office. The interior of
a Union starship was generally regarded as the safest place
to be outside of a member planet's surface or an outpost. It
was, however, a reasonable precaution. Claire had insisted
on conducting the psychological examination free of intru-
sion. Adam was traumatized enough as it was. A one-on-one
probe would ensure the greatest potential for progress.

Adam sat stiffly on the couch directly opposite Claire,
looking and feeling grossly uncomfortable in his standard-
issue civilian clothing. His face appeared exhausted,
defeated, shell-shocked. As confident as she was in her training and her judgment, Claire knew these were nonetheless
uncharted waters. The situation was unprecedented, and
must be treated as such, with circumspection, sensitivity, and
extreme caution. There was no reason to risk accidentally

contributing to the destabilization of a brain that already appeared poised to unravel. Recovery would be a long haul, and gradual, incremental growth was the goal.

"I know this must all seem . . . utterly unreal," she said to him, in the gentle, authoritative manner that made her so naturally well-suited for this job, "but I'm here to help guide you through the transition. Any thoughts, any feelings, questions, fears . . . I want you to express them all."

Otto glared back at her with an expression that suggested something in the vein of I would cut your throat if I had a knife.

"Where are my wife and child?" he hissed softly, the ship's translation matrix smoothly converting the arcane German dialect into decipherable speech. It was the tenth time he had demanded an answer to the question, and although Claire understood all too well the feeling of separation from family—she recalled the experience of being isolated from her children, Ty and Marcus, while stranded on a desolate alien world after their shuttle had crashed—her awareness that Annelise and Alger had been mere simulations colored his appeals, creating the impression of an obstinate child who insisted upon having the same story read to them each night.

"I'm . . . I'm very sorry. I know it's painful. But you have to understand . . . they weren't real."

Despite her legendary calm, Claire was startled as Adam leaned forward and spat at her, his saliva speckling her cheek and the deep green of her medical jacket. "You are trying to trick me," he snarled. "It will not work. What have you done with them?"

"They were part of the simulation," she answered, casually wiping off the moisture as if such attacks were a regular occurrence.

"How were you able to drug me without my knowledge?"

"I promise you, Adam, you're not drugged—"

He shot to his feet, and Claire briefly glanced toward the security officer stationed outside. "Stop calling me that!" he shouted furiously, a vessel bulging and throbbing in his temple. "A Jew's name! My name is Otto!"

"You believe . . . you're under the influence of a narcotic. That this is a hallucination. Is that it?"

"It can be nothing else! In Germany we have experimented with such things. No doubt the Allies have as well. I promise you that you will get no information from me! I will die first!"

"Would you . . . sit back down for a moment?" she asked gently. He glared at her, but he too was aware of the guard's presence, and evidently had no immediate desire to engage. After a few seconds of visible internal debate, Adam begrudgingly acquiesced, though the polar glint in his eye remained targeted.

"Thank you." She smiled. "Now, put your hand on that cushion. Feel the couch you're seated on. The texture. Feel it? That's it. Good. Now, the floor beneath your feet. Feel its hardness. Its solidity. Do any of these things seem illusory to you?"

"They are figments. And so are you."

"You're in a sickbay. I'm a doctor. Even in the world you know, those things should be familiar. Start there. Use them to anchor yourself." She knew the naval vessels of the twentieth century were, in a way, Old Testament patriarchs of today's faster-than-light starships. Perhaps Adam could summon the vision to connect the dots on a rudimentary level.

He regarded her with a cold sneer. "A Schwarzes doctor?"

"All right, let's try finding another way in. You were shot. Do you recall that?"

"Yes."

"The bullets passed right through you. Do you remember?"

"Yes. . . ."

For the first time, Adam's steely resolve and self-assuredness began to show spiderweb cracks. Had she found a keyhole into his besieged psyche?

"How do you think that happened?" she pressed. "How did those bullets pass right through you without causing harm?"

"They . . . did not," he said, his face growing pale.

"What do you mean?"

"I was shot. And killed." For the first time, he looked at her without malice. In fact, much like the holographic bullets, his gaze appeared to pass right through her.

"I am . . . I am dead."

Although the *Orville*'s command structure was not democratic, Captain Ed Mercer was predisposed to evaluate the opinions and recommendations of each of his top officers when it came to the weighing of complex decisions. On this morning, they were all present, gathered in the conference room to discuss the next steps in the handling of this decidedly anomalous scenario. The question at hand: What to do with Adam?

"Are the Colliers going to face charges for illicit research?" asked Talla, her security officer's mindset zeroing in on the legal ramifications.

"I wouldn't expect a life sentence," said Kelly. "Both the Union Council and the Admiralty feel that given the . . . unusual circumstances, and the amount of time that's passed, the charges, if any, will be light."

"This is an utterly unprecedented situation," Ed reminded them with a perturbed sigh. "There's no rulebook. Even the Union Council is divided, so for the moment they're kicking it back to us, since we're the ones who are out here in the thick of it."

"Lazy bastards," muttered Gordon, the *Orville*'s jocular, red-haired helmsman, rolling his eyes.

"Any and all opinions are welcome," said Ed, opening the floor to comments.

Claire was the first to chime in. "Well for the moment, he

hasn't accepted the reality of his circumstances. Until we cross that threshold, he's still my full-time patient. After that . . . I'm not sure what happens."

"And of course, there's the elephant in the room," said Kelly.

"That is a false statement," said Isaac, his luminescent blue eyes glowing from behind a quizzically cocked silver-toned cranium. "There is no such pachyderm."

"Someone'll explain it to you later, Isaac." Kelly plowed ahead. "The fact is . . . for all intents and purposes . . ." Her words hung in the air, though they all knew how the sentence ended.

"The guy's a Nazi," said the ship's navigator, Charly, her bullish bluntness outsizing her diminutive appearance, as usual.

"To the core." Kelly nodded, the expressive curve of her long neck moving in emphasis of her statement. Talla and Bortus, the *Orville*'s formidable Moclan second officer, had required a crash course in human history, but the rest of the room's biological occupants knew the context well from their school days. Centuries ago on Earth, when the planet's land masses were still sliced up into subsets of individual sovereign nation-states, each one regulated by its own independent governing body, intraplanetary conflicts were frequent, with various militaries striking out at one another periodically in their quest to control desired areas of land or unchecked possession of natural resources. Occasionally, one of these nation-states would become powerful enough to send a ripple of influence across the globe, affecting the coexistence of the planet's inhabitants as a whole. A small country called Germany had accomplished this during the middle of the twentieth century. The regime had been harsh, brutal, and even genocidal in its practices. Millions of people were rounded up and exterminated because they did not meet the bizarre genetic purity standards of the nation's rulers.

"As far as Adam's reality is concerned," Kelly went on, "he has participated in one of the most notorious massacres in Earth's history."

Gordon scratched his scruffy, close-cropped orange beard with a thoughtful squint. "Yeah, but . . . it was a simulation. No one really died."

Kelly nodded. "That's the wrinkle."

"So . . . what happens?" asked Charly. "Does he get treated as a war criminal or not?" She had directed her question to Ed, who remained silent. The intensity of her blue-eyed stare made him suspect that she was perhaps drawing mental parallels to another, more recent massacre. Charly Burke had lost someone very close to her in the battle with the Kaylon. The wound was still fresh, and perhaps she viewed this case as a sort of surrogate for a past war that could not be refought.

"Okay, let's say Dr. Finn rehabilitates him," she continued. "Let's say he gets to a place where he understands what's happened to him. What then? You can't just let him go free. He's dangerous. Even if the people he killed were holograms, it doesn't matter. He believed they were real. He's a psychopath."

"That's the thing," said Claire. "He's not."

"What do you mean? Look at what he did!"

Claire, as always, responded to fire with the coolness of a university professor. She explained patiently in her low, musical voice. "After Earth's Second World War ended, there was extensive research to determine how so many people could have been persuaded to commit the premeditated, methodical murders of what was simply called 'The Holocaust.' It was statistically impossible for all of them to be insane. It just couldn't happen. So something else had to be at work. What the research revealed was far more chilling: These were regular, ordinary people, who had simply fallen in line behind a voice of authority. Even though it meant the mass extermination of their fellow human beings."

"And the worst part of the discovery," Ed added with sobriety in his voice, "was that the instinct is inside every one of us. Waiting for a skilled demagogue to harness it. Picture yourself in Adam Collier's shoes. I'm sure you think you'd resist the authority of your superiors if they instructed you to kill. Maybe you would resist. But the research suggests that for most of us . . . that's a fantasy."

"What happened to him could have, and most likely would have, happened to any of us," said Claire.

For the first time since the conference had begun, the deep rumble of Bortus's bass-toned voice was heard. "Those who succumb to such moral weakness must still be held accountable."

"Without question," affirmed Ed.

"He must go to prison," Bortus's deep voice rumbled.

Kelly shrugged. "Where?" It was a good point. There were no real prisons in the twenty-fifth century. The term was used colloquially, but the institutions it referred to were just rehabilitation facilities. Around the year 2215, humanity had made peace with the fact that prisons themselves were largely inefficient societal tools that, though they were designed to turn out citizens, usually instead manufactured criminals, and that other, more complex and evolved means of behavioral correction offered the dual virtues of being both more humane and more effective. There really was no standard mechanism in this century to contend with someone like Adam, who was, in every way that counted, a man from another time. "And what would you charge him with?" she added. "Killing simulations?"

"Hell, we've all run combat programs in the simulator," Gordon pointed out. "I guess that'd mean we should all face charges."

Ed leaned forward in his seat, hands clasped together and brow furrowed. "It also depends on what you believe the primary function of a prison is. If it's the punishment of the offender, then yes, we should lock him up. But if it's merely to protect society, or to serve as a deterrent to future offenders . . ."

Chief Engineer John Lamarr emitted a small snort. "What future offenders? The last Nazi died centuries ago. He'd have a tough time selling the idea to anyone in the twenty-fifth century."

Gordon glanced at the glittering stars that dotted the infinite void outside. "Has he . . . looked out a window yet?"

"No," Claire said. "The sickbay windows are obscured."

"Is it a crazy move to . . . just show him around the ship?" asked Talla, though her expression suggested limited confidence in the wisdom of what she had proposed.

"At the moment," Claire answered, "it could overwhelm him. Possibly even send him back into shock. He needs to be eased into the actuality of his new world somehow."

Suddenly, Gordon's face brightened and he sat up straight. He turned to Claire with an almost mischievous smile.

"I have an idea."

CHAPTER ELEVEN

The title cards proudly blared their text, buttressed by the Wagnerian explosion of trumpets, heralding their proclamation: *Universal Pictures Presents: FLASH GORDON! Starring Buster Crabbe, Jean Rogers, and Priscilla Lawson!* Gordon and Claire paid no attention to the names of the long-dead entertainers, but were instead focused on the audience: Adam Collier, who stared transfixed at the screen in front of him. Ed and Kelly observed from a discreet distance as Adam slowly ran his hand back and forth through the image, which hovered just above the control pad on Claire's desk.

"How . . . does it float?" he asked, mystified.

"It's a holographic projection," said Gordon excitedly. "But that's not what's important. What matters is what's on it."

A cartoonishly antiquated 1930s-style rocket ship flew through space, its complement of three passengers fuzzily visible through the scratchy black-and-white grain of the film upon which the images had been captured.

"It won't be long now, eh, Flash?" said Dr. Zarkov. "There's ol' Mother Earth coming up to meet us."

"Where do you think we'll land, Dr. Zarkov?" asked the fetching Dale Arden.

"Can't tell exactly, Dale. But I hope it'll be a large, open space."

"Anywhere but the ocean," offered Flash Gordon himself.

Adam appeared to lose patience. These images were arguably outdated even in his own "time." He glared sharply at Gordon. "Why do you show me this?"

Gordon responded with the characteristic warm enthusiasm that had made him such a well-liked, popular member of the *Orville*'s crew. "Well, this idea that . . . that we could someday travel through space . . . on a . . . ship of some kind . . . I mean, it's not so far-fetched, right?"

Adam did not respond. He appeared to be searching Gordon's expression, trying to determine what subterfuge was being employed here, and to what end.

"Well, is it?" Gordon pressed.

"I suppose not," Adam answered flatly. Gordon glanced at Claire, waiting for approval to continue. She gave him a solemn nod.

"Okay, what if I told you . . . you're not dead."

Not a single facial muscle strayed from its position as Adam looked stonily at the *Orville*'s helmsman.

"You're actually . . . on a spaceship. Not quite like the one in the movie, but still a spaceship."

"Preposterous," said Adam flatly. He almost sounded bored, as if he were in the hands of third-rate interrogators who couldn't even lie convincingly.

Claire had been studying Adam's reactions with the intensity of a hawk, and she surprised everyone the room with her next move. She gently placed a hand on Adam's elbow, and said, "Come with me."

As she guided him out into the main sickbay, they realized what she intended to do. She gestured subtly to the guard, who dutifully backed away, but stood ready to intervene if anything went south. Claire stepped over to the far wall, where the sickbay windows had been sealed to obscure the reality of what lay beyond.

"Come here," she said. It sounded more like a request than a command, and as Adam was unrestrained and unshackled, he appeared to see no downside to playing whatever game was unfolding here, if it meant gathering more information about his captors.

He approached the window. Claire nodded to Kelly, who gently pressed a touch pad on the wall. The coverings slowly retracted, and the blackness of space, the rhinestone speckling of stars near and distant, and the great spinning ellipsoid of the planet below suddenly engulfed his field of vision.

It was as if all of his confidence, all of his self-assuredness, and all of the animal paranoia and suspicion that hobbled the twentieth-century mind were instantly leveled by the force of the impossible. He froze. His knees looked as if they might buckle, but he remained upright. His trout-mouthed expression would have been comical had the circumstances been less severe. For the first time, his biting tone became subdued, and he spoke softly.

"God in heaven . . ."

From the moment Adam had been revived inside the sickbay of the *Orville*, his world had been confined to the space within its walls. He had been aware that he was being detained in a facility that was advanced far beyond even what Germany had developed (or at least what he was aware of at his limited level of security clearance), but he had been utterly unprepared for the enormity of what now lay before him.

He was led out of his confinement into a long, glossy corridor that appeared to be constructed of unfamiliar metals. It was impossibly sleek and refined, with mysterious lighting fixtures that, though they were placed overhead, seemed to bathe all corners of the structure at once as if their luminosity traveled through the very air. The whole effect was otherworldly. The doctor, along with the ones called Ed and Kelly, as well as two members of their security detachment, guided Adam down the corridor toward an elevator of some kind. Once inside, the doors shut with a smooth, quiet whoosh, and a soft humming sound told him they were on the move. It was, however, the only clue that they were no longer stationary. There was no sense of instability, no trace of the slight gravitational upset that always accompanied a ride in a lift. Just smooth calm. Almost immediately, the doors opened again, and another corridor lay ahead.

"This way," said the one called Ed. They rounded a corner, where a grand-looking spiral staircase ascended toward another deck. When they reached the top, the shock and terror that had only just begun to abate returned in full force. The corridor above opened up into a command center the likes of which no one could ever have imagined in the wildest tales of fiction. A vast viewing port looked out into space beyond . . . but he barely noticed it.

The place was full of horrific creatures that looked as if they had emerged from the fiery depths of hell. What could only be described as a monster, incongruously dressed in the same blue that Ed and Kelly wore, turned suddenly to face him. Its degree of deformity was abhorrent. Its head was grotesquely misshapen, with multiple ridges protruding from the cranium, and the contours of its brow, cheekbones, nose, and chin looked more like the features of a nightmare beast from a child's fairy tale than anything human. Beside the creature sat a woman who looked like a demon incarnate. Her face was strangely alluring, but the long scales lining her forehead and sharp-tipped, malformed ears sent a shiver down his spine. At the other end of the large circular enclosure was a man with no face. His entire body was covered by a hard silvery shell, and his features were nonexistent save for a pair of eerie glowing, blue orbs where human eyes should be. Adam felt dizzy and sick to his stomach.

"What . . . is this place?" It seemed as if he could barely hear the sound of his own voice over the rush of blood in his ears. Was it possible that this was hell? Had Germany's quest for purity and his participation in such through the exercise of mass liquidation been a gross error? He had, occasionally, in the privacy of his own thoughts, confronted dark apparitions of doubt—not about the Führer's great plan, but rather the methodology that he and those like him employed in its execution. Could it be that God had sympathy for the Jews? It seemed an inconceivable hypothesis, and yet . . . these creatures were not of his world.

A new voice from behind interrupted the tempest of thoughts. "You're on a starship, Adam."

He turned sharply, his military mind still acutely alert, reacting as an involuntary muscle.

They were two strangers he had not met since his ordeal had begun. They were older, perhaps sixty or sixty-five. They did not wear the odd, brightly colored uniforms that the others wore. But they were human. In this upside-down, phantasm-fueled madhouse, that was at least something. They regarded him with peculiar gazes. The others had seemed cold, analytical, probing—as if he were an animal in a zoo, or a prisoner himself in one of the camps. These two, however, were different. Their expressions were almost . . . caring. Loving.

"Adam . . ." said the woman, taking a cautious step forward, one hand outstretched toward him, "we . . . we are your parents."

He felt something inside him snap. All fear and trepidation suddenly converted to rage, pouring itself into his bloodstream like he was being force-fed. Whether it was God himself, the Allies, or some other unknown enemy manipulating his reality, it was going to end here and now.

"Enough of this trickery!" he shrieked. "I want to see my wife! My child! Where are they?! If you've hurt them, I swear to God I'll kill you all! Where are they?!" He tried to bolt back down the corridor, but he was firmly grasped by the two security officers. He thrashed about, bellowing furiously. "Annelise! ANNELISE!! Let me go, God damn you! ANNELISE!!"

"It's okay! It's okay," said the doctor, trying to rest a hand on his flailing arm. "We'll take you to her! All right?"

He stopped. She spoke softly now.

"We'll take you to your family."

CHAPTER TWELVE

The doors parted to reveal the stark, empty interior of the *Orville*'s environmental simulator. Claire and Adam stepped inside, followed by Talla and her two-man security contingent. Both she and the guards knew full well that her Xelayan strength was more than adequate to subdue a single human male should he become violent, however the increased security presence was meant as a deterrent, to prevent the likelihood of resistance in the first place. Ed and Kelly remained a discreet distance behind the rest, along with Leonard and Pamela, who had begun to look as though they were running treacherously low on sleep.

Claire could see in Adam's widening eyes a mixture of fear, hope, and recognition. He must have had some dim, warped understanding that this room, familiar as it now was, could be the portal back to his own world. She moved to the panel and addressed the ship's computer.

"Begin simulation."

As always, the very molecules in the air appeared to shimmer, and the momentary sense of disrupted equilibrium that accompanied the transition from the real to the imaginary gave way to a crystallized image: They were back in Poland.

It was the very parlor in which Ed and Kelly had first visited "Otto Vogel": quaint but well-appointed, with the smell of cooking sausages filling the air. And there in the center, with an oddly placid smile on her face, showing rows of sharp, white, simulated teeth, stood Annelise. She held young Alger in her arms as she gazed with artificially generated affection at the man who had loved her with such genuine passion.

At the sight of her, his broken constitution suddenly appeared to re-integrate, like a moving picture of a fallen building played in reverse, restoring its shards into solid form.

"Annelise! Alger! Thank God!"

He ran to her. "Have they mistreated you? Are you all right—?"

But when he reached her, his body passed right through hers, sending him tumbling to the floor, just as he had back in the camp. He staggered to his feet, stunned, and immediately pivoted to try again. And again he pitched forward, finding no purchase from the apparition. Instinctively, Pamela moved to help him, but Claire silently gripped her elbow, shooting her a look that said it all: He has to get there on his own.

This time, when Adam rose to his feet, he simply stared at his wife, in a stupor of sorts, and tremulously extended a hand to her cheek. Of course, all he caressed was empty air. And then, at last, a pre-dawn realization began to shine the first rays of its light upon his awareness. He looked again at the smiling face of the woman he loved, and for the first time, he saw her as something very different.

The smile was a hollow, ironic, pitying smile—not cruel, but not warm. To Adam's eyes, there was now an emptiness there, almost as if he was looking at a faded photograph instead of a living, breathing, flesh-and-blood woman. And while he did not yet truly understand how these illusions had been created, he began to process their true nature: They were phantoms. Echoes.

"Annelise..."

He fell to his knees.

"No..."

Claire watched with a combination of deep empathy and clinical relief as he huddled there, pressing the heels of his hands into his eyes, and wailing. She nodded to Pamela. It's all right now. The two of them approached the crumpled, diminished figure, and Claire knelt down beside him.

"I'm sorry," she whispered. "They're not real. They never were."

— ✧ —

Ed Mercer strode purposefully through the corridors of his ship, making sure to take in, as he always did, the astonishing beauty of her construct. The day he had been welcomed aboard by Admiral Halsey, who had given him this, his first command, he had silently vowed never to stop appreciating its technological artistry, and never to take it for granted. He loved the *Orville*—her shiny brass-colored corridors, her expansive windows affording breathtaking views of the cosmos from everywhere on board, her grand spiral staircase that opened up into the spacious world-within-a-world that was the command bridge, the elegant curvatures of her hull. He was proud as hell to be her captain, and he knew the thrill would never get old. Yet even within this familiar, homey environment, surprises inevitably lurked.

As he approached the guest quarters, Ed was momentarily thrown by the presence of an armed security guard posted outside. It took him a split second to recall that, of course, he had ordered the guard's presence himself, however it was decidedly irregular for such an extreme protocol to be enacted aboard a starship, and the reflexive part of his brain had instinctively reacted with perplexity. This was home base, a safe territory, which, under normal circumstances, did not require such visible precautions.

Ed nodded to the guard, and hit the door chime.

"Come in," said a voice from inside.

The door whooshed open, and he entered the room. Claire was seated on the sofa with Pamela and Leonard, who, though their faces indicated that they were as lost and confused as ever, at least appeared to have managed a bit of rest. Claire rose to her feet. "Captain."

"How's he doing?" Ed asked.

"He's . . . made some progress."

"How much?"

"More than I'd hoped for, actually. He's beginning to understand that, as alien as this world may be . . . it's the real one. I suppose we're lucky that the simulation was the mid-twentieth century as opposed to the Middle Ages or ancient Egypt. He at least had the advantage of living in an age of relative reason and scientific literacy. He seems to understand that we're human. Could be worse. A twelfth-century man, for example, might have come to the conclusion that we're gods requiring propitiation."

Ed looked to Pamela. "Does he understand that you're his parents?"

She turned away from him with a weary look, and a quivering lip.

"It's hard to know at the moment," said Leonard. "He won't answer any of our questions. He'll barely even speak to us."

Ed waited an appropriate beat, then asked gently, "May I try?"

Although he was their son, Leonard and Pamela looked instinctively to Claire. A week ago, she would no doubt have advised Ed to afford Adam Collier the care and delicacy with which one might handle antique china, but now she simply nodded.

Ed approached the bedroom door, with slight reservations about his own motives. At least for the time being, it was his job to assist in the shepherding of this man's adaptation to the world of the twenty-fifth century. However, if he were truly honest with himself, a selfish anthropological curiosity was also at work here, partially driving this encounter. While Adam Collier was not a thawed-out Neanderthal brought back to life from a prehistoric era, nor the result of some anomalous temporal displacement wave like the one that had ensnared a younger Kelly Grayson from seven years into the past and thrust her into the present, he still represented a once-in-a-lifetime opportunity for cultural observation. If perhaps not in actuality, Adam was, in all the ways that mattered, a relic from a bygone era. For anyone, historical expert or otherwise, it was almost irresistible. The twentieth century—hell, even most of the twenty-first—had been a period of tribalism, paranoia, and division. It was an odd hybrid of great leaps forward in terms of technology and scientific growth, combated by a desire from many cultural corners to maintain a viselike grip on the ways of the past. It was something of a marvel that the human species managed to squeeze through this narrow hole of history, and to emerge on the other side ready to embrace its own future: a future that would eventually blossom into the galactic wonder that was the Planetary Union.

When he entered, the first thing he noticed was that Adam had shaved. Ed wasn't a psychiatrist, but it seemed to him that attention to grooming was a good sign of mental stabilization. The man stood facing away from him, staring out the window at the fluttering light of the distant and not-so-distant stars.

"It's quite a view, isn't it?" said Ed, benignly.

Adam did not answer, and did not move.

"You can't see Earth from here, but I can point out a few stars that have planets a lot like it. Interested?"

Again, he did not answer. Ed was about to shift tactics when Adam suddenly spoke.

"Does Germany still exist?"

While a perfectly predictable inquiry for a man of his era, it was somehow, with all this galactic splendor on display, not the first question Ed was expecting. It was absurdly small, inconsequential. Nonetheless, he was careful with his answer. He wanted to encourage this hard-grained artifact of a man to be open and honest, without veering toward complaisance himself. You couldn't just stretch out a hand in friendship to a Nazi.

"The . . . architectural and cultural history of Germany still exists. There are plentiful records of its past, and no shortage of literature available on the subject. But . . . it's not quite the way you remember it. Earth is now a single, unified, global civilization. With all kinds of people working together."

Adam emitted what could either have been a prolonged

sigh or a low growl, and closed his eyes.

"Then we failed."

Ed took a cautious step forward. "How so?"

"We fought a war to secure Germany's position as the dominant ruling power in Europe. And someday, perhaps, the world. We did not succeed."

"Adam," said Ed patiently, "the war you were fighting was lost centuries before you were born. This is a brand-new world. And . . . if I may say so, a better one. I think you'll be pleasantly surprised if you open up your mind a little."

"Do you work with Jews?"

"Why do you ask that?"

For the first time, Adam turned to face Ed. A look of disgust dripped down his face like melting butter. "Your doctor. She is a Schwarze. I have seen others here. If you employ such creatures, perhaps you also employ Jews."

This was a hard one to explain thoroughly to a man out of time. The world that was so routine and ordinary to Ed was utterly mint-new to this man. Ed tried nonetheless. "The fundamentals of your question presuppose a cultural separatism that is . . . irrelevant in this century."

Adam brimmed with hostile impatience. "Are there Jews?"

"We no longer slice up our identities in that way," Ed responded calmly. "We are one species, working in tandem with hundreds of other species as part of a larger Planetary Union. It's just . . . different than what you know."

There was a silent moment, then Adam sat down on the edge of the bed. "You speak as though you believe you have built a utopia. When in fact, all you have done is pollute yourselves."

Ed was beginning to get a taste of what daily life must have been like four hundred years ago, rife with grandiose drama over stakes that now meant nothing.

"If you can put yourself in the other guy's shoes," he said, "you can walk a lot farther. That's what we've found. And it's what your Germany failed to grasp."

"You allowed them to breed. To infect."

"That's the computer talking."

Adam cocked his head in a way that, had it not been tainted by such a confused, defensive, derisive expression, would almost have reminded Ed of Isaac. "The computer?"

"Try to understand this," Ed explained. "Your entire worldview has been shaped by a machine blindly executing an algorithm. There was no conscious effort to persuade you of any specific ideology. The computer was simply responding to your actions and decisions, and adjusting its program accordingly. It was trying to service you. It even protected you from real danger, real pain." A flash of inspiration burst across Ed's mind. Risky, but inspired. "In fact . . . you've never felt pain, have you? No, of course not. The safeties were on the entire time. For your entire life you've been shielded."

"I have felt pain."

Ed, even more resolved now, took another step closer.

"You think you have. But the simulator doesn't allow a user to be hurt beyond a superficial degree. Haven't you ever been … punched? Kicked? You ever cut yourself? Never really put a dent in your day, did it? But you must have seen hurt happen to others. Didn't it ever strike you as odd that you were spared?"

Adam tensed as Ed drew still closer. "Stand up," Ed ordered. He was met with nothing but a look of defiance. "Stand up if you're really a soldier."

Adam snorted with dismissal. Chin high and swagger in force, however, he rose. The second he was secure on his feet, Ed swung. Adam went down like a sack of potatoes, twitching on the floor for all the world like Lieutenant Yaphit. He suddenly looked like a stunned, wide-eyed toddler who has taken a hard fall but has not yet begun to cry.

From Adam's perspective, it was indescribable. The most horrific feeling he had ever experienced. It felt as if his own body was turning against him, gnawing at his face from inside, consuming itself. He tasted something strange and oddly salty on his lip. His tongue darted out of his mouth, probing for the source, and found wetness. Instinctively, he put a hand to his mouth, and pulled it away, examining the findings. Blood. He looked up at Ed, feeling real fear. What otherworldly power was this? Was it a weapon? Who were these people? And how could they be capable of such malevolence?

Ed looked down at Adam Collier, and felt pity. But the

lesson was done. "Understand this: That's a mosquito bite compared to what you did to those people. Or what you thought you did."

He walked away, returning to the living area.

"Maybe he'll talk to you now," he said to the Colliers. But his confidence in his words was low. He opened his mouth to say more, but thought better of it, and departed in silence.

CHAPTER THIRTEEN

Adam lay flat on his back, staring up at the featureless ceiling of his cell. For that was how he viewed it—not only the room, but also his new universe: a prison from which he could not escape, no matter how far he might travel. He was weary, but unable to sleep. He had asked one of the security officers to help him obtain some German litera-ture in the ship's historical archives, and had managed to locate *Mein Kampf* in the original Deutsch, but his brain could not focus, and he soon found himself reading the same passage over and over without making any sense of the words he was seeing. What little rest he had managed was haunted by dreams in which he felt trapped, suffocated by thick, malevolent air, from which his lungs could extract no oxygen. At last he rose again, and for what seemed like the hundredth time, shuffled and drifted around the room aimlessly, mind numb, soul empty, silently moving about the stultifying environs as if he were his own ghost.

Enough.

He walked to the bedroom door. Obediently, it opened. There was no one in the outer room. Cautiously, Adam moved to the main door, and took a deep breath. He began pounding furiously. "HELP! HELP ME! I'VE BEEN HURT! PLEASE, HELP!" He then darted to the side, flattening his back against the wall beside the entryway. Presently, the door slid open, and the red-uniformed security guard stepped inside. The guard barely had time to react before an elbow slammed into his jaw with a sickening CRACK! The guard went down. For all the veritable centuries that divided them, fortunately for Adam a man was still just a man. His military training served him well as he finished the job, pummeling the guard into unconsciousness, taking satisfaction in the act, after having been treated as a fragile antique for so many days. He plucked the sidearm from the prostrate figure, and examined it closely. The intricacies of its operational mechanisms were alien to him, but the shape was familiar enough. When he held it in his hand, he found it in fact not dissimilar to the military-issue Luger he had once carried.

Adam stealthily crept out into the corridor, his watchful eyes alert for enemies, his body poised for combat or flight. He was alone. Finger on the trigger of the weapon, he hastened toward the T-junction ahead. Peering around the corner, he spotted a young woman in orange, eyes fixed on a small glowing object of some kind, from which she appeared to be reading. Occasionally she would tap it a few times, and it would emit a small burst of sound. Adam retreated behind the corner, and lay in wait. After a moment, she reappeared in view, and with lightning-quick agility, he leapt out and grabbed her, clapping a hand over her mouth, and pressing the barrel of the weapon to her temple.

"The . . . simulator!" He hissed, saying the strange word aloud for the first time. "Where is it?!"

He carefully pulled his hand away to allow her to respond. "I . . ."

"Where is it?!" He pressed the weapon harder against her head.

"That—that way," she stammered, awkwardly pointing back the way she had come.

"Show me. And if you cry out to anyone, I promise you will die." He roughly pivoted her body a hundred and eighty degrees, then gave her a hard shove, stuffing the weapon into the waistband of his trousers. Still shaking, the woman advanced down the corridor as Adam followed.

They passed a few other crew members, most of whom were too occupied to clock any suspicious dynamic in the passing pair. One young man in green gave them a second glance, and Adam's nerves tightened for a moment as he readied himself to extract the weapon. The man, however, evidently decided there was nothing odd about the uniformed officer and her civilian companion strolling down the corridor, and moved along without interfering. Adam silently marveled with disgust and disdain at the apathetic protocols that allowed military officers to walk about unarmed. He probably could have accomplished this without the weapon.

They approached the large double doors marked Environmental Simulator Three.

"Open it," Adam commanded. The woman worked the small pad on the wall to the right of the doors, and they slid apart, revealing the stark, silvery interior. Adam smashed a fist into the woman's face, knocking her out cold. He stepped over her slumped form, and entered the chamber.

What now? He moved to the small interior panel, and stared at it anxiously. What was it the doctor had said to summon his world before? He couldn't remember. With frustration, he slapped a palm against the panel.

"Please state request," uttered the antiseptic, expressionless voice.

He spoke aloud to the empty air, his own voice echoing inside the vast cube. "I . . . want to go home."

"Please specify parameters."

He did not know what this meant. And the longer he delayed, the greater the danger his captors would find him and stop him before he could return home.

"Home!" he cried frantically. "I want to go home! I am Otto Vogel! And I want to be with my wife and my child!"

"Please specify timeframe."

He blinked in confusion. And then it began to crystallize. Was it conceivable?

"Time . . . time . . ." He sifted the possibilities in his mind. "Ten years after the war. With Germany victorious. We have a beautiful home, in the Bavarian countryside. We are happy there. Annelise, Alger, and me. That is where I want to go."

The air shimmered around him . . . his equilibrium was momentarily disrupted . . .

. . . and then he was home.

It wasn't the home he had known in Poland, but rather a new place, unfamiliar and yet inviting nonetheless. Sleek, streamlined-looking furniture filled a spacious, airy living room, with a chandelier above that illuminated the dwelling via glass balls that looked like a cross between a snowflake and a star. A wooden box with an inset screen stood in the corner, two thin wires protruding from its top. On the screen, a well-groomed man was reading the news items of the day. Television. He had heard about it being used in 1936 to broadcast from the Olympic Games in Berlin, where Hitler himself had given the commencement speech, but the technology had clearly advanced by the time, which must be the mid-1950s. But far more glorious than any of these novelties was that his wife, Annelise, sat comfortably on the olive-green sofa, her petite legs crossed beneath the hem of a charming pink housedress, a warm, loving smile on her face as she rose to embrace him. And in that moment, he knew for certain that this was where he wanted to stay. This . . . beautiful fantasy. It didn't matter that it was not real. He would rather live within the protective womb of his dearest of illusions than out there, in the unforgiving real world.

"Welcome home, darling," she said silkily as she wrapped her pale white arms around his neck and kissed him long and hard. She was eager and alive and flushed with color from a day in the summer sun. As he pulled away to admire the bottomless blue eyes of which he had been deprived for so long, he caught a burst of movement in his peripheral vision. Turning to the front door, beyond which a lush green lawn with a majestic oak tree was visible, he saw a handsome young man of about sixteen enter from the outside. The face was familiar.

"Alger!"

"Hello, Papa." The boy grinned.

Adam spun to grab the lad by the shoulders. "Stand there. Face me." What a fine specimen of unsullied Aryan-Nordic breeding! This was the future for which Germany had fought. "Look at you! You're practically a man!"

He pulled wife and son into an ecstatic embrace, as he gazed once more at his surroundings. "And this . . . this is our home. We are home!"

Annelise laughed. "Of course we are, darling. Where else would we be?"

As he reveled in the luxuriant idyll of the world he had restored and ushered to its most decisively supreme potential, he became aware of the voice coming from the television set.

"The Führer announced today that General Gerhard Abendroth will succeed Minister Von Ribbentrop as First

Reichmaster of the United States." The screen showed an image of the White House, looking as it always had in films and photographs Adam had seen, with one significant alteration: The swastika fluttering nobly in the breeze above its columns.

"Minister Von Ribbentrop will oversee the conclusion of normalization procedures in South America, where the few remaining resistance cells have at last been crushed. As his final act as Governor General of the United States, Ribbentrop will oversee the official installation ceremony of the newly completed Monument des Führer, which stands proudly in New Frankfurt Hafen, formerly New York Harbor." The picture shifted to reveal a breathtaking image of a colossal, towering iron statue of Adolf Hitler, right arm raised in salute, looming tall where America's Statue of Liberty had once stood.

Everything was exactly as he always knew it would be. This was the grand future they had been promised by the Führer, come to pass before his very eyes. Did it really matter if it was a . . . simulation? Perhaps the truth could be different for everyone. This was his truth. He felt as if an oppressive weight had been lifted from his shoulders.

As he placed his hands on Annelise's warm cheeks and bent his head to kiss her again, Alger suddenly turned away, startled. A hole opened up in the far wall. Beyond it, the corridors of the *Orville* were visible. They were here. He reached for the weapon still tucked into his waist.

Talla fired. Her aim was as true as ever, and the blast hit Adam square in the chest. He fell to the floor, stunned and unconscious.

"Papa!" cried Alger, rushing to his father's side.

Annelise looked at the Union officers in terror. "Who are you? What have you done to him?"

"End simulation," said Ed, and mother and son dissolved into nothingness.

Talla approached Adam, easily picked him up, and carried him out the door. As Ed watched the limp features move by, he was struck anew by the tragedy of the man's life: an abandoned child thrust by chance into the care of a mindless machine, which had unwittingly led him down a long and perverse winding path of indoctrination toward this day, when all that remained was a mass of hatred and shattered hopes.

CHAPTER FOURTEEN

Adam had not resisted when they put him aboard the shuttle. He had appeared listless and small, and as depleted as an empty quantum core. He had not even required sedation. Gordon dutifully prepped the shuttle for departure, with Talla along for the ride just in case circumstances deteriorated again. Underscored by the low, heavy thrum of the shuttle bay, Ed, Kelly, and Claire stood with Leonard and Pamela Collier, saying their muted goodbyes.

"Captain, thank you for everything you and your crew have done for us." Pamela dabbed the last traces of moisture from her damp eyes. The sight of her son shuffling listlessly and without recalcitrance toward his fate had spurred another effluence of emotion.

"I wish we could've done more," said Ed sympathetically.

Leonard looked intently at the *Orville* officers. "I haven't wanted to ask you this, but . . ."—he sounded pained as he forced the words out—"if he *can't* be rehabilitated . . . what's going to happen to him?"

"He did assault two officers," said Kelly, hoping it wasn't too brusque. "They've both recovered, and they don't want to make an issue of it. But he *will* need to be placed under guard for a while. After that, only time will tell."

Pamela shifted uncomfortably. "And what about his . . . other crimes?" It had been the unsolvable puzzle since the day Adam had arrived.

"That's as much a question for the philosophers as for the courts," said Ed. "If his crimes had been real, he'd face the consequences. But the fact is . . . he wasn't an actual participant in the atrocities of Nazi Germany. That happened almost five centuries ago. Adam's world was fiction, and no one has been hurt. Except, of course, Adam." This answer felt oddly empty, and seemed to satisfy no one. Ed felt sorry to leave them without any kind of equilibratory anchor to better make sense of what had happened to their son, but he was at a loss. "I guess it just depends on your opinion of the fundamental nature of wrongdoing: Is a crime defined by the act itself? Or by the harm it does to others? If you can resolve that conundrum, then you have your answer."

"The Melbourne Center is one of the best on Earth," Claire assured the Colliers. "If anyone can deprogram him . . . they can."

"Dear God, I hope so. I truly hope so," said Pamela softly.

"I'm sorry for everything that's happened," Kelly said. "If

there's anything else you need from us, please don't hesitate to ask."

"Thank you. I'm sure we'll be fine."

Claire put a comforting hand on Pamela's arm. "Mr. and Mrs. Collier, if you're so inclined, and if it's not too much trouble . . . drop us a message now and then. I'd like to know how he's doing."

"We will," said Pamela, offering a wan smile. As the Colliers trudged up the ramp and into the shuttle, Ed was struck by the incomparable loneliness that they must be feeling. To lose a son or a daughter to accident or disease was a tragedy, but in a dangerous universe, it was an experience as common as it was profound. A parent didn't have to look exceptionally far to find a sympathetic ear from someone else who had endured the same trial. What had happened to the Colliers' son, however, was something altogether different. Their boy had been taken from them, but he was still physically present, trapped in a sort of living psychological death from which no one yet knew if there was hope of escape. They would receive no empathy or understanding from other families grappling with the fallout of the same relatable crisis. They were on their own.

EPILOGUE

The peach pie flooded the bakery with hot aromatic sweetness as the old man set it gently on the countertop. As he moved away to allow it to cool, he took a moment to survey the interior of his establishment. He had been here some years now, however he still marveled at the creative hybrid of twenty-sixth-century technology and old-Earth classicism that the architect had achieved. It was very much emblematic of his life as a whole, and the long and unique journey he had endured before arriving here at this quiet destination with its peaceful sense of finality. He had recently turned ninety-five, and he fully expected to live out the remaining decades of his life in the tranquil serenity of this place, surrounded by the one vestige of his origins that still had value.

The ovoid door irised open, and a customer entered. He was tall, around seventy-five, with dark skin, smiling eyes, and a gentle face. The man looked around the shop, taking visible pleasure in the offerings he observed there. He approached the counter. The old baker wiped his flour-covered hands on his apron, and addressed the younger fellow.

"Good day. May I help you?"

"I'd like a loaf of cinnamon bread." The man's voice was a rich baritone that hit the ear pleasantly. The baker reached under the countertop, and retrieved one of the fresh loaves displayed behind the glass. He placed it on the counter, and began covering it in a cloth wrap.

"This is a quaint little shop," said the customer.

"Yes, we've been here for quite some time."

"I've heard this place was here, but I never stopped in." The man smiled appreciatively as he watched the old baker methodically wrap the loaf. "Smells good. You know, you don't find too many people nowadays who know how to bake. Especially with the technology . . . you can't tell the difference between the real thing and the synths anymore."

The baker looked up sharply. "*I* can tell."

"Of course. I didn't mean to trivialize it. I'm just impressed. Where'd you learn to do it?"

"My . . . father taught me."

"Family business. Nice to see."

The baker finished wrapping the cinnamon loaf, and handed it to the kindly customer. "Will there be anything else?"

"No." He paused thoughtfully. "Well, actually as

curious . . . I think . . . I think you knew my mother. Years ago."

"Did I?"

"On the *Orville*. Dr. Claire Finn."

"Oh . . . yes. Yes, I did. She was very kind. She . . . helped me through some difficult times."

"Yeah, that sounds like her. She was a pretty extraordinary woman. My name's Ty. Ty Finn."

"A pleasure." They shook hands. Ty took the loaf and put it under his arm. "Well, thanks for the bread." With a smile and a nod, he turned and departed. The ovoid door irised open, and he was gone.

The old man returned to his baking. There was much work still to do.

ACKNOWLEDGMENTS

Seth wishes to thank: Brannon Braga, André Bormanis, Jon Cassar, David A. Goodman, Joy Fehily, Alana Kleiman, Tom Costantino, Cherry Chevapravatdumrong, Jason Clark, Howard Griffith, Andre Danylevich, Andrew Nagorski, David Shapiro, Bill Sienkiewicz, Bruce Boxleitner, Jim Jackoway, Karl Austen, Eric Weissler, Anthony Mattero, Marie Ambrosino, Sung Park, Cassy Brewer, Kelli Gallagher, Chris Bartholet, Jennifer Kessler, Adam Wilson, Dan Kaufman, Tonya Agurto, Carol Roeder, Jennifer Levesque, Amy C. King—and the production and audiobook teams at the Disney Publishing Group, and all the incredible cast and crew of *The Orville*.

ABOUT THE AUTHOR

S eth MacFarlane is a five-time Emmy-winning, Academy Award–nominated and Grammy-nominated actor, writer, director, producer, and singer behind some of today's most popular entertainment content. At twenty-four, MacFarlane became the youngest showrunner in television history when his animated series *Family Guy* aired on Fox. The show, which recently celebrated its twenty-fifth anniversary, has garnered him five Emmys and makes him the co-record-holder for most voice-over Emmy wins of all time. MacFarlane also created and voice-acts on the fan-favorite animated series *American Dad!*

Through his production company, Fuzzy Door, MacFarlane wrote and directed *Ted*, *Ted 2*, and *A Million Ways to Die in the West*, and produced Paramount's recent *The Naked Gun*. He and Fuzzy Door have since expanded the Ted franchise with two series for Peacock—the live-action prequel series and the animated series of the same name—in which he reprises the voice of the iconic foulmouthed teddy bear.

MacFarlane also hosted the eighty-fifth Academy Awards—where he was nominated for Best Original Song for *Ted*—and *Saturday Night Live*. With a deep appreciation of the Great American Songbook, he has released nine critically lauded studio albums, including his most recent, *Lush Life: The Lost Sinatra Arrangements*. His musical portfolio has garnered him five Grammy nominations and several No. 1 iTunes Jazz Charts debuts. Through his Seth MacFarlane Foundation, he is an avid supporter of science communication, cancer research, climate conservation, free speech, and equal rights for all.